Voices
from the
Sand

CYNTHIA PELMAN

Grosvenor House
Publishing Limited

Cover photograph by Justin Sholk
www.justinsholk.com

This book is published by
Grosvenor House Publishing Ltd
28-30 High Street, Guildford, Surrey, GU1 3EL.
www.grosvenorhousepublishing.co.uk

A CIP record for this book
is available from the British Library

ISBN 978-1-78148-870-6

Also by Cynthia Pelman

Joshy Finds His Voice

DEDICATION

This book is dedicated to all grandmothers.

To Granny Sylvia D., who taught me that it is hard to feel love when you are hungry.

To Granny Gertrude M., who told me that even though her life has been brought low, her grandchildren, who she is bringing up because their parents have died, will be 'up there, up high', because they are learning to read.

To my own Granny, Sheindel Kolnik, who in 1904, at the age of 12, created a library in a little village in Eastern Europe.

And to my mother, Freda Sholk, who was a very special granny to her grandchildren and showed them the preciousness of books.

* * *

The book pays tribute to the pioneers of Cognitive Education, including Carl Haywood, David Tsuriel, and the greatest of them all, Reuven Feuerstein of blessed memory.

I hope that any errors in my interpretation of their work will be forgiven, and that I have got it right, at least in principle.

* * *

'He raises the poor from the dust,
The needy from the refuse heap,
Giving them a place alongside princes.'

Psalm 113

'Clear the road for my people,
Pave the way,
Remove the obstacles.'

Isaiah 62.10

CONTENTS

PREFACE

You ask me to tell you about myself.

It's okay, you don't need to apologise for asking me all these questions. Here I am being interviewed for a job at this bank, in an office. And office work is something I have never done before.

So I can see why it seems surprising to you. It is a bit surprising to me too.

And it is a question which even people who know me well, my husband and my friends, are asking me. They say to me, Dolores, why would you, a teacher, want a job in an office, where you will be sitting at a desk with a computer all day, counting money not children?

So maybe if I tell you about myself, where I have been working, and some things that have happened over the years to me and to people living in our town, in Sandveld, it will help you understand why I think I have had enough of teaching, and why, after twelve years in one job, I am ready for something different.

And maybe afterwards, you will tell me what you think of my story, because I know that people who are not from South Africa have read a lot about us, about apartheid, and our new democracy, and about poverty, but I think a person who has not lived in a place for a long time can't actually know what it is like, what we have gone through and what we have achieved.

* * *

PART ONE

Noticing and Naming

CHAPTER ONE

My name is Dolores.

I am a teacher.

I am a Coloured woman.

For us, this word 'Coloured' has a different meaning from the way you people in Europe and America use the word 'Coloured'. I have been told that you use that word to mean anyone who is not White.

But here in South Africa, to be a person who is called Coloured is to be a person who belongs to a specific people, a minority group, just one of the many groups or cultures in this country. We are not a big group, tiny in fact if you compare our numbers to the much bigger Xhosa or Sotho or Zulu nations.

We are people who are a mix. We descend mainly from Malay slaves who were brought to the Cape by European settlers about three hundred years ago, but we descend also from the native Khoi-San people, who were the original people living here in the Cape before anyone from Europe arrived. We have some Black ancestors, mostly from the Xhosa nation, and a little bit of White, from those Dutch and English and French farmers who came to settle in the Cape over three hundred years ago. We speak our own version of Afrikaans, although most of us also speak English. We have special foods we like to eat, and traditional songs. Some of us are Christian, some are Muslim.

We have our own history and identity. We are not White and we are not Black.

That was always something a bit unusual, because you probably know that here in South Africa people were very concerned to keep each nation separate from each other nation, and in those days the idea of mixing people from different groups was not only shocking, it was also against the law. But in spite of that, here we are, a mix of bloodlines and colours and religions and languages.

We have gone through some things which are very specific to our community and I think it is completely different from the experiences of Black or mixed-race people anywhere else in the world.

* * *

Let me tell you about my work and what I have been doing all these years since I left Teacher Training College.

I teach at the Sunbeams Preschool in Sandveld, on the outskirts of Cape Town, and I have been working there for the last twelve years. I have a class of thirty-six children. They are four years old, and I teach them every day from 8.30 until 2.00. We try to teach them well, so that when they get to 'big school' they will be able to learn properly, to read and write, not like most of the people of my generation.

People are calling my generation the lost generation. A long time ago, in 1976, Black children in Soweto started student riots against apartheid. You may have heard of this. The idea spread to all the cities and townships in South Africa. Some of those children died, some were put in prison, but all of us got shaken up and life wasn't the same after that. I was only three when it started, but a few years later, by the time I was seven or eight or nine, I knew how to listen and I knew what it meant when one afternoon, it was in 1983 I think, my cousin Eddie, who was getting involved in that stuff, came home limping, hiding his face, and it turned out he had been on a protest march and the police had shot him with birdshot and he had deep little wounds down his arm and one on the side of his face. Some people were not as lucky as Eddie and had much worse happen to them.

So people at that time, especially teenagers, had other things on their mind and school was not something that they were thinking about. Eddie never did go back to school, he was too angry, and he has stayed an angry person to this day.

I suppose because I was a bit younger it was easier for the family to make sure I kept going to school. I don't know what I would have done if I was a teenager in those years when it all started. I wonder if I would have joined in the protests, but I don't think I am a brave person really, and anyway I didn't have to find out because when I was a teenager my family kept me under such strict control and observation I would have had to break with them totally to get involved and I was too timid to do that. I know I could have done more. But some of that stuff we don't talk about.

Anyway, I was telling you about my work. I teach at Sunbeams every day, and after the school programme ends at 2 o'clock, only a few of the kids go home. Most wouldn't have anywhere to go to, because their parents are at work. And some of the parents who are not working, and that is lots of them in Sandveld, can't look after their children for other reasons, and don't have enough food to provide three meals a day. So I stay at the school and run the after-school programme for the children who have to stay here all day. We give them lunch, they have a nap. We look after them and wipe their noses and play with them and make sure they don't get hurt.

How long have I been in Sandveld? I first came here sixteen years ago looking for my mother. I was eighteen then, still at school. Don't think I was a young child with nobody to look after me. I was not a lost child. When I was a child, right up until I finished school and started college, I lived with my granny, Grandma Rachael, my mother's mother. She brought me up from the day when I was four years old and my mother disappeared. My mother was the one who got lost, not me.

I came to live in Sandveld a year after I found my mother, who had landed up here after having travelled all around the country. She never really told me where she had been all those years. I lived in Sandveld for six years until I got married to Johannes and I moved to his house in Retreat. Now I am thirty-four and have a child of my own, my Elise, who is now eight years old, and I still wonder how it was that my mother could disappear and not come back. Even though I know that life sometimes does things to you that can break your spirit. I have seen it in my own family and I have seen it here in Sandveld. I asked her a few times, she gave me a different answer each time, and sometimes she just got cross because I kept asking. After a while I stopped asking. Now we see each other nearly every day, and I am happy to be near her. She is really old these days, she doesn't see so well, and I can make sure she eats something every day.

Anyway, during those years when I lived with Grandma Rachael, one of my uncles told me that he had heard that my mother was living in Sandveld. Grandma Rachael did not approve of my asking about my mother. "*Los dit my kind!*" she said. "Leave it alone! Your mother made her choices a long time ago. Don't you have a good home here?"

Grandma Rachael never wanted to talk about my mother. "She made a decision, leave it at that," she used to tell me. "This is your home, you can stay with me always. We will look after each other, you and me."

And, of course, I had the best home with Grandma Rachael. At her house, there was always food in the kitchen, even when she didn't have regular work after the clothing factories started closing down. The house was clean and tidy, she and I did the cleaning and cooking at home together and she taught me how to do it, and we used to sing while we were cleaning because she said, "Some things in life are just boring, but if you sing, you can make it *lekker!*" I remember all those songs, '*Daar Kom die Alibama*' and '*Nee nee nee madola*'.

Grandma Rachael made sure I got to school safely; she walked me to school and from there she went to work, and after school when she was still at work she made sure our neighbours kept an eye open for me when I got home and made sure that I wasn't dawdling in the street. Sometimes Grandma used to take me to the market and we used to browse, looking at the beautiful fabrics, the shoes, the sunglasses. She tried to help me with my homework even though she didn't really like reading or writing, especially not in English, and she listened to my sob stories about girls who were mean to me, or about nasty teachers who asked us ridiculous questions.

And there were always other people in the house, uncles, aunts, friends of the uncles and the aunts, and neighbours popping in all evening after work. So we were never alone, it was never quiet, it was warm and busy and lively and crowded.

We lived in Woodstock, not far from what used to be called District Six. When District Six was cleared out by the Government, and everyone had to leave and the houses were demolished so that no Black or Coloured people could ever live there again, some of us Coloureds were allowed to stay on in Woodstock. I think the authorities made a mistake with their paperwork and their lists, because everyone else was being told to leave, but somehow a few of us kept our houses and stayed. I have heard it said that they allowed us to stay because some parts of Woodstock were so windy, directly in the path of the North-Easter wind blowing gales right over the mountain, that no Whites wanted to live there anyway.

Everywhere else where Black and Coloured people used to live, like District Six, Claremont, Sea Point and Simonstown, got emptied out of Coloureds and Blacks and they were all sent to live in places like the Cape Flats where nobody knew their neighbours and the wind blew the sand over those endless dunes and houses were plonked down in rows, all the houses the same, and there were no trees, and no colours, no mountain, and no familiar faces.

Just in case you think that Grandma Rachael and her family were clever to choose Woodstock as the safest place to live, as if they knew it would be one of the only places Coloureds would not be evicted from, I'll tell you that it was just luck. And also, when I was doing my teacher training course we had to do a personal history project and I researched the history of Woodstock and found out that until 1834, slaves were bought and sold, and sometimes hanged, under a tree called the Treaty Tree, right there in Woodstock where we felt so safe. So maybe there is no such thing as a really safe place.

* * *

Anyway, I had this urge, something pulled me to find my mother. So one day I took a bag of sandwiches and some money for the taxi and set off for Sandveld. Well, it's a long story and maybe I will tell you about it another time, but I found her, and I stayed with her for a while and we made our peace. Grandma Rachael was very upset and she refused to come and visit, and I missed her a lot. I went back and forth, from Sandveld to Grandma Rachael, and we would sit on the *stoep* in Woodstock and talk about old times. I didn't want her to think I wasn't grateful for the home she gave me, and I missed her scolding and her philosophising and all those times we cleaned the house and sang, and I even missed hearing her telling me that I should stop dreaming and get down to doing some work. But I wanted to be near my mother.

Grandma Rachael died five years ago. She never spoke to my mother from the day my mother ran away until the day she died. But I think in the end she understood why I had to find my mother and why I came to Sandveld.

When I went to England in 1993 on a student teacher exchange scholarship with teachers from the UK, people there were shocked to hear my story about my mother. But here in South Africa it is nothing special. Here in South Africa most people have a sad story about their family. Everyone's family got broken or removed, everyone lost their house and their neighbours, and nearly everyone has someone in their family who is ill or is on drugs or who was in jail or who disappeared.

You ask me, do I like this country? I don't think about like or don't like when I think about this country. I live here. It is our place, we know who we are here.

And it is a funny thing, when you are part of a small group, a minority, it makes you know exactly who you are and where you belong, because you never have the feeling of being one of millions, of being indistinguishable in a crowd. There are so few of us, and we are so obviously not Black and not White. So I feel proud of who I am: I am a Coloured woman.

CHAPTER TWO

When the wind is blowing in Cape Town you start to seriously respect the power of nature. Roofs blow off, ships are driven against the harbour wall, cars veer onto the wrong side of the road, and surprised birds land up looking forward but flying backwards.

And when the wind blows in Sandveld it gets right in your face. Here we have no trees, no gardens, no lawns to keep the dust down. Some of the roads are paved, but the others are dust tracks. And that sand doesn't stay put, it wants to get up off the road and visit everyone in their homes and in their eyes and ears and mouth. After a windy day in Sandveld you need to sweep your floors and wash your head under the tap to get the sand out of your hair.

Sandveld is a township built on the beach. Not the usual kind of beach, mind you. When you think of a beach you probably think of deckchairs, brightly coloured sun umbrellas and people eating ice cream. That is not the kind of beach you have in Sandveld. In the days before roads and buildings, Sandveld was just sand dunes. Now it is a place where a lot of people, from many different places in Africa, speaking many different languages, try to live out their lives and keep their children safe.

The wind sweeps in on an unbroken path from the South Pole, across the Indian Ocean, into False Bay.

It makes land on the coast just in front of Sandveld. In some public buildings in the area, special roof fixings have had to be used to make sure roofs don't blow off in the South-Easter gales.

Here you have to take special care when putting up a building, because otherwise heavy machinery gets stuck in the sand. Only last year, when they started building the hall for our new primary school, this really did happen, and it took half a day to free the huge crane which had been brought in to put up the steel supports.

The builders had erected a huge sign saying 'New School for Sandveld' with the name of their company in big letters, and it was quite funny really, in a sad way, to see their sign, with its sturdy steel legs, bent over by the gale so it looked like an old man with a bent back.

This wind used to be called the Cape Doctor, as it was supposed to be able to blow away plagues and diseases. But at the moment it seems that in spite of the wind our plagues are here to stay.

***

It was on one such windy day that I first met Devlyn. He was new in my class. Everyone else had started at the beginning of the school year, but he arrived a month later.

All children are a bit shy in a new place, and it takes them a while to get used to the place and to the other kids and to the teachers and the rules of a school. But Devlyn was different right from the start. For one thing, he was really small. He looked like a child of three, and compared with some of the older kids in my class who were already nearly five, he was tiny. Not just short, but thin. His wrists were so skinny that they looked like the wrists of a doll.

It wasn't just that. Even after he had had time to settle in, after about a month, by which time I expect a new child to start to learn, to enjoy playing and to listen when I read a story, Devlyn was somehow different. He didn't seem to listen, didn't seem to be able to focus on any one thing for long. He would sit and watch us for a while, and give his sweet smile if someone spoke to him, but he didn't really respond. It is hard to explain; he just seemed somehow different from the others. He was, in some way I couldn't explain, apart. Not unfriendly, not distant, but not really participating in anything.

He seemed so fragile, not solid. I sometimes thought if the wind blew too hard while he was in the playground he would just be blown away and we would never see him again.

I would watch him and try to see what he enjoyed doing, what caught his attention. Usually I had only a few seconds to observe him before he moved on again, maybe stopping briefly to look at some children doing a puzzle, then to look at something on the wall, then on again. He reminded me of a *mossie*, you know, those little brown sparrows which you see everywhere in Cape Town; always on the move, always slipping away from one place to another. So small that sometimes they are almost invisible.

I wondered how old he was; perhaps they had him in the wrong class? He looked so much younger than the other four-year-olds. But I checked in the file for his date of birth and he was four, like the other children in my class.

Devlyn had a constantly runny nose, so I thought maybe it was ill health which made him so different. But lots of the kids in my class have runny noses, and in spite of that they don't usually look ill, they are lively and energetic and love singing and dancing and running around. Devlyn didn't sing, he seldom joined in when we danced, and only spoke in response to being spoken to. I wondered if his hearing was the problem, as lots of small children, when they have colds, also get fluid in their middle ear and it gets blocked there and causes infections and then they don't hear well. But he did seem to hear everything – he would look around if someone came into the room, he would notice if someone dropped something on the floor. He was definitely alert and could hear. Maybe too alert. Even a bit jumpy and nervous sometimes.

What struck me most, looking at Devlyn, were his eyes. His eyes were constantly on the move: looking around, looking behind him, looking at the windows, looking at other children and what they were doing. But not really stopping to look at any one thing for long. It felt like he was always watchful, looking out for something which might come from any direction.

On his first day, he had been brought to school by his mother, a petite, very thin woman who spoke hardly at all. We told her that as he was new she could stay with him for a little while, but she didn't seem to want to and she left quickly. She came to fetch him quite early, though – we had told her she could come back at 2 o'clock, but at noon I saw her standing outside the school gate waiting for him. I sent someone to ask her to come in, but she refused and stayed outside the gate, with a baby tied with a blanket on her back, for almost two hours, until the school day ended.

* * *

After that, Devlyn would be dropped off by his mother on time every morning but she didn't come and pick him up after school. He was one of eight or nine kids who were picked up after school by Granny Sophie.

I have to explain to you about Granny Sophie. Sophie is a big woman in every way: tall, statuesque, solid, with a big, outgoing personality. She owns the Shebeen next door to our school. A Shebeen is more than a pub: its doors are open all day and most of the night, and it provides a meeting place, a place where people can talk and relax and drink home-brewed beer.

In apartheid days, pubs and bars were not open to people who were not White, and the traditional women's role of brewing beer, and Sophie's extravert personality, made opening a Shebeen an easy choice for her. Lots of women in South Africa start up little businesses, they call it the informal sector, and you would be amazed how many women are totally self-supporting here. These days, since the end of apartheid, it is easier for Black business people to get a liquor licence, and many Shebeens are now legal businesses.

Sophie is a big, motherly woman who looks more like a comfortable, stay-at-home granny than the clever businesswoman that she is. Her home-brewed beer is held in high regard by her customers, and though it is one of several Shebeens in Sandveld, she has her regulars, as well as the group of kids that she takes care of.

This is how it happened that a Shebeen owner is also a child carer. Many of our parents need to leave for work in the city very early, before the school has opened its doors. So either they must get to work late or leave their children alone in the house and just hope that they will get to school safely on their own. Sophie had a brilliant idea and let it be known via her client network (and most of them go and have a drink at Sophie's Shebeen some time or other during the week, so they all heard what she had to say) that she would be willing, for a very small fee, to look after the children from the time their parents had to leave to catch the bus; she would take them next door to Sunbeams as soon as the school doors opened, then pick them up after school so they could wait with her until their parents fetched them. And so it came to be that Granny Sophie has at least seven and sometimes even more children sitting in the Shebeen in the early morning, and she carefully shepherds them to school and makes sure they go in and are received by one of the teachers before going back to tending her beer and her more adult customers. In the afternoons, at 5 o'clock, she collects her children, making sure they have not forgotten their jumpers or shoes, and takes them next door to wait in the Shebeen for their parents to pick them up an hour or so later.

I know it sounds ridiculous, maybe even wrong, to have seven young children start and end their school day at a Shebeen. But here it is not considered so unusual. The children are perfectly safe, and it is just another sign that Sophie is a strong woman who knows how to get things done.

And so Devlyn settled into the classroom routine, and went to the Shebeen with Sophie every afternoon and would be picked up there by his mother in the evenings and taken home.

We didn't know if his mother worked, and we didn't know what she did all day while Devlyn was at school, but we sometimes saw her walking around Sandveld with her baby tied onto her back with a blanket. She lived on the outskirts of Sandveld, in the squatter camp called Overcome Heights, so none of the parents of our kids knew her.

I decided to try to spend more time with Devlyn. I would set the children a task, maybe drawing or cutting and gluing, which I knew would keep them busy for a little while, and I would go and sit next to him. He seemed to enjoy this and he always gave me the sweetest smile. He was always well-behaved, always fitted in with the class routine, never disrupted anything, and his attendance record was perfect: he had never missed a day of school in spite of his constantly runny nose. But he didn't really do anything and didn't seem to learn anything.

CHAPTER THREE

In its early days, Sunbeams was just a crèche: a safe place for a child to spend a few hours, perhaps play with other children, get a good meal and have a sleep, while their parents went to work. It was built by the Sandveld Development Trust from some old shipping containers which had been welded together. The space between the two rows of containers was roofed over to make a big corridor, really wide, and we use that middle space as an extra room. On Sundays it is rented from us and used as a church.

During the week we use the middle space for singing, because you can fit all the children in and it has a good roof so in summer they are not too hot and in winter they stay dry. In winter it is not warm, though – there is no heating and the metal walls are not insulated. The wind howls through that corridor, going in one end and out the other, blowing the sand in so that we need to keep sweeping it out every few hours. But it is dry.

At the end of that corridor we have a tiny kitchen, just a corner with a sink and a cooker, and our cook Bertha makes lunch for the children there. We also give them breakfast: the Salvation Army come every morning with a white van and two enormous pots of hot porridge and two strong men to carry the pots into the kitchen. We give each child a plate of porridge with milk and the pots get picked up later. That way we manage to give each child two meals a day. I don't know how it is that the Salvation Army came to be giving us breakfast every day but we are grateful for it.

* * *

We also have a dog who comes to school every day. The dog belongs to nobody but he thinks he lives here. He sleeps on the pavement at night when he gets chased out and we lock up, but in the morning there he is, waiting for me when I unlock the gate and the front door. He slips in and finds a spot to lie down out of the wind. He is no trouble, he just sits or lies there most of the day, scratching his fleas and flicking his tail when the flies get too bothersome. We once had a flock of goats coming in too, they seemed to think that once the gate was open we would welcome anyone and anything, and we had to shout and hit spoons on pots to get them out. But the dog stayed.

These days Sunbeams is more than a crèche, because the people who fund us decided they want the kids to have a proper education programme and they hired some qualified teachers, like me. So now we like to call it a 'pre-school', even though it is still a place where we change nappies, where the kids can have two meals and a nap, and where we keep them safe during the day.

Originally we only had the shipping containers, with kids grouped in three different classes according to age and one container kept for the office of our school principal Frances. Later we got two more classrooms built, in a brand new brick building whose costs were donated by some very kind people. The brick classrooms are a bit bigger, and have properly insulated walls and big windows, but the container classes are small and dark, and they have twenty or twenty-five children in each class. With a chair for each child, and a table for every six children, there is little room for anything else.

***

Sandveld is next to a big highway. On the other side of the highway, not on our side, there is a suburb where wealthy people live, mostly Whites. They have really big houses, with lots of rooms, and gardens with flowers and trees, and each house has a front door as well as a back door. The back doors open onto the *vlei*, the lagoon, and some people have little boats and they go rowing. I know that because a lady who lives there has been visiting our school and helping us teachers in all kinds of ways; she is a very experienced teacher herself. And once she invited us to her house for a *braai*, a barbecue.

Also, some of our people from Sandveld go across the highway to work for those people, cleaning their houses or doing their gardening, and they tell us about what they have seen there, so we know how different those houses are from ours.

Every morning, from about seven o'clock, if you stand near the highway, you will see streams of people coming out of Sandveld and crossing the highway. Some are walking to work in the big houses, and others work further away and have to cross the highway to get to the bus or the train. But you will hardly ever see White people crossing the road in the other direction, coming towards us from their side. It's one-way traffic only in the morning.

***

When I finished school I went to train at Teacher Training College. It seemed like the best thing at the time, because although I wasn't such a good student at school, and my teachers would usually write in the school reports 'must concentrate more' and 'needs to stop dreaming in class', I actually liked school, especially seeing my friends and being with them all day. Anyway, I didn't have any other ideas at the time and Grandma Rachael believed that a teacher is always respected in society and will always be able to find work. And at college I did okay, though I spent a bit of time doing some political stuff, which I don't want to talk about, and I didn't always work too hard. I remember Grandma saying to me, "Dolores, *meisie*, my child, if you would just stop dreaming for a bit and do your homework, there will be plenty time for dreaming afterwards."

All the women I knew, the women in my family and their friends and our neighbours, worked in the clothing industry. The factories were not too far from where we lived, and before the evictions the women would walk to work together and walk home together. After everyone was thrown out of District Six the women had to travel for at least an hour to get from their new houses in the Cape Flats to work, but still, it was a place of regular employment for thousands of women.

It was safe, steady work, no surprises and no worries. But the whole group thing put me off. I couldn't imagine walking to work and spending all day, having lunch, walking home, with the same people you see next door and on the weekend, and every summer evening when you sit on the *stoep* to get some cool air. Talking about the same things day after day, having the same experiences with the same people. It kind of seemed suffocating to me. I wanted to see new things, to go somewhere, to start something different.

Maybe I am a bit like my mother, always wanting to go and see something new, only she went somewhere and never came back. All I did was go to college to become a teacher.

Anyway, I am still the same, I still don't like being in big crowds with lots of people and I never fitted in with the group of girls at school who were sexy and popular and who walked around in short skirts, flashing their eyes at the boys, and it was the same at Teacher Training College. I was usually on the side of the action, not in it, with one or two friends, no more. Or just sitting on my own and dreaming.

Maybe there are two kinds of people. Some like to be in big gangs, to do things together, and that can be good, like our neighbours who used to support each other and like the friends who were always around to give a helping hand, but it can also be bad, like those gangs which our young people are so caught up in. But the other kind of person is like me, I suppose, people who prefer to be on our own, on the side, thinking our thoughts.

* * *

Sunbeams Preschool, where I work, and also the Sandveld library which is just down the road from us, are run by the Sandveld Development Trust. The people on the Trust are local people who have been working for years to organise the community, and they have the help of a wealthy businessman who lives in a mostly White part of Cape Town and who has for the last ten or more years been advising them on how to run the Trust like a business, with proper accounting for all the money coming in and all the money spent. So the Trust keeps careful watch on what we are doing at Sunbeams, and they are determined that our kids will get the best possible education, even though we are a poor township where lots of people don't have work, and where many adults can't read or write very well.

Last year, out of the blue, the people from the Trust had a meeting and they asked Frances, the principal of Sunbeams Preschool, to talk to me afterwards. She told me that they wanted me to go and study some more.

They didn't mean that they were not happy with my work, which is what I thought at the beginning. They weren't trying to tell me that I didn't know enough about teaching. What they were saying was that they wanted to be sure that the children at Sunbeams get the best possible preparation for going to school. They had read that if children's education is postponed until they are six years old and they then start school, they don't do as well as other children who have had an earlier start. They also said that they had been visiting other schools in Cape Town, private schools which are attended by children of wealthy parents, and one in particular called Silverleaf School, and they wanted our children to do as well as the children of Silverleaf were doing. They wanted our kids to have the same chance of doing well at school as those kids in private schools.

We all know that Black and Coloured children of this new generation need help. They don't do so well at school. Many of them can't really read or write even when they finish school, and because of this they don't find jobs, even in the new South Africa where jobs are open to all races. So when Frances told me why they wanted me to go and study further, this was nothing new to me. I am a teacher, so I know the problems. And don't think we teachers are okay with this thing: most of us know something has to change, something has to be done, and we know it is up to us.

But we are not sure what to do. We work hard, we do everything we were trained to do, and still, so many kids drop out, so many end up in trouble, and so few get jobs. It is as if a curse has been visited on our nation: to be poor, and to stay poor.

The donors from the UK who fund our preschool came to visit, and took the people on the Trust to visit Silverleaf nursery school, to see how they do things. They told the Silverleaf teachers about Sunbeams, and those teachers invited us to come and visit them any time we wanted to, and to share in any training they were getting. Those teachers are getting extra training all the time, all kinds of courses, and that is how they help their kids to be clever and to start school already knowing how to read, how to add up, how to sit still and listen.

So the people from the Trust told me that they wanted all the Sunbeams teachers to learn the most modern things about teaching, but we couldn't all go at the same time because Sunbeams had to keep functioning while we were studying, so only one could go at a time and I had been chosen to be the first.

And that was not all: they also said that if I wanted to, and if I could do it in my own time, in the evenings, they would also pay for me to go to university to do a post-graduate course in a special teaching method, called Cognitive Education.

The people from England also told me about their dream to build a new primary school, and that they had collected the money from donors overseas, mostly in the UK, and would be starting to build in a few months. Our school, Sunbeams, could send all our kids straight on to the new primary school.

I got really excited. Until then, all the children who left Sunbeams nursery at age five had always had to go to schools which are some distance away; they had to cross that big highway and walk quite a way, in winter or summer, and it was not safe. And now there would be a local school, in our own town, so kids could go safely to school and which the Trust would be supporting to make sure that they had the best teachers and the best opportunities to learn.

It was a new start for me, too. At age thirty-three to go back to university! Who would have believed it? I wished Grandma Rachael had been around to see me now – she would have been so proud of me! I had finally stopped dreaming long enough to do something serious.

CHAPTER FOUR

Around the middle of the year we got another new child in the class. That made thirty-six, and our class was now full up. The school rule is that no class can have more than thirty children, but I don't remember when we had only thirty, it is always more.

Our new child was Isaac, and he was a burns child. It happened in his previous house, in another township, not here in Sandveld. When he and his family came from Malawi they had nothing, no jobs and no money, so they lived in a shack with some other people, and his mother had no place to cook food, other than the one room where they lived. Isaac was two when it happened; he was not yet stable on his feet and the room was crowded, and he went too close to the table on which the hot water was standing, ready for cooking, and pulled it over himself when he stretched his hand out to balance himself. He was now four, and his file said he had had seven operations so far and would have to have more.

More children are burned in South African townships than you would believe.

He wore a hat to cover the scars on his head, but the scars and deformities on his face couldn't be covered. He had bandages on his right hand from his most recent surgery, so he had to use his left hand for everything, which must have been hard as it said in his file that he was right-handed. But his legs were fine and he could run around in the playground just like any other child.

Isaac's family had moved to Sandveld recently and now they had a bit more room, sharing a house with another family but at least there was a separate cooking area, so hopefully the children in the house would be safe from burns now. But Isaac still had a long way to go.

Because of all his operations he had missed out on at least a year of schooling, so we decided to put him in my class of four-year-olds, even though he was already five. We didn't want him to keep missing out on learning because he would have to go into hospital for more operations every few months, so we thought at least let's make it easy for him at school, let him just have fun and play.

I sat with him when the children were drawing, and talked to him a little. He didn't know any Afrikaans yet but spoke quite good English, and I was impressed by his confidence and his easy way with talking. I asked him if he liked to draw and if he could draw with his left hand, and he said, "I used to draw lots, but now my hand is in this bandage. But I can do it, slowly-slowly." And he took a pencil with his left hand and drew me a shaky picture of a boy and a ball.

He talked about it with such matter-of-fact acceptance. I don't know if I could do that. Maybe we adults have learned to tiptoe too much around difficulties, and we try so hard not to stare, not to upset people, but kids just say things as they are and get on with it. I have to say I was shocked when I first saw Isaac, but after a few days he was just another one of my kids, and what's more the other kids in the class didn't notice anything special, just asked him why he always wore a cap, and he explained, and that was that.

* * *

Meanwhile, Devlyn was still worrying me. He was so cute, adorable really, with his big smile, his teeth somehow too big for his little face. But there is no place for cute and adorable in township life. You have to be tough and you have to be smart. Already some of the bigger boys tended to tell him to get off the slide if they wanted to get on and he would just make way for them.

Of course, he was still only four, but I could just imagine him, in a few years, still small, still cute and smiling, not able to stand his ground or protect himself in the tough life of a school playground or when walking down the road.

I spent some time with him every day. I just wanted to get to know him, to see what else he could give me besides the smile, to see if he could sit still and get a job done without being told what to do. I gave him simple tasks to begin with. "Devlyn, *kom hier my kind*! Come here my boy. Can you help me tidy up these books? The kids left them on the floor, let's put them away on the shelf, nice and tidy. Big ones here, small ones here."

Without a word, he would flash his smile and do everything I asked him to do. Then he would just stand there, waiting for another instruction. If I said nothing he would wander around the classroom, doing nothing much, just looking around.

One day I decided to see if he could think of something to do without me telling him. I said to him, "Devlyn, *kom*! What do you want to do?" He just stood there, looking at me, with a little smile. I tried to be a bit more specific, to give him a hint. "Is there anything we should tidy up? Anything in a mess? Maybe we can clean up somewhere?" But he just stood there.

It's not that he didn't understand what I was saying, because when I said, "Maybe we can wipe the tables, where the children were painting? It's so dirty on the tables!" he immediately understood, fetched a cloth and started cleaning the tables.

It was this passivity, his not really connecting with what the others were doing, not joining in, which got to me and which worried me. Would he agree to do anything that an older person told him to do? What would that mean for his safety? It wasn't only that he seemed unable to initiate anything on his own; he seemed unable to think for himself at all. How do you teach a child like that to stand up for himself and to say no?

From one dreamer to another. Maybe that's how Grandma Rachael felt about me when I was a kid.

***

The wind was particularly bad that week. We had a South-Easter, which is what we call our really vicious wind, and it just blew and blew for days and everyone's temper was short and we couldn't keep the sand out of the classroom and the kids' eyes. On one day we tried to keep the kids indoors at break time but the classrooms are so small, it was so crowded and the kids needed to let off some energy, so we let them out and they ran around in the wind with their hands protecting their eyes from the sand and crashing into each other and having a marvellous time.

But that sand reminds me of something that happened in Sandveld a few years back, something that will maybe give you an idea of the kind of thing we live with here.

A while ago, actually it's a few years now, a builder who needed sand to mix into his plaster or his concrete or something came to Sandveld and he wanted to buy our sand.

Now, anybody can see we have too much sand, more sand than any town could ever need. The only problem was, nobody in Sandveld knew who should be dealing with this builder because who knows who is the owner of sand? One of the tough guys in our town muscled in because he wanted, of course, to get the money, and our Sandveld Development Trust had a huge argument with him because they thought the money should go to them, to help develop the town and to support the most needy people. In fact, we found out later (though maybe the people involved already knew) that the sand actually belonged to the City Council.

Anyway, there were arguments and threats and blackmail and bribery and in the end the builder did get truckloads and truckloads of sand, and he got it at a really cheap price so we felt that he had stolen from us. Not that we need the sand. What we need is trees and water. But he got something, a part of the earth, that made a lot of money for him and we got hardly anything. And the fighting that happened was ugly and quite scary for some of the people involved.

It's not that different from what I read recently about how big companies mine oil or diamonds or minerals from the earth in countries which are basically poor and not well developed. I don't know anything about how it works, I don't understand the economics, but

I know that some of those countries are left as poor as they were before they started producing the oil or the diamonds.

After that thing with the sand and the builder, I was sitting with the other teachers and watching our kids at break time and staring at the sand which was the cause of so much trouble, and we suddenly realised that maybe all this sand that everyone was fighting about could have some use after all. We had been just ignoring it and wishing it would lie still, but maybe we could do something with it?

We started throwing around ideas, and we got sillier and sillier. Let's bake cakes with it! Let's use it to teach the kids to count, we've got so many grains of sand that we can get up to really high numbers! Let's dig a pond and get some beach chairs and invite tourists to the Sandveld Beach Experience! But there were some really good ideas too.

And so we made percussion instruments from old plastic water bottles with some sand and stones inside, and had a music session; we had a treasure hunt where we buried small toys in the sand and the kids had to find them; and we mixed sand into pots of paint and made a lovely thick gloopy mixture which the kids used for finger painting. We mixed sand with cornstarch and cold water and the kids could build sandcastles that didn't just collapse and blow away. We took empty plastic water bottles and put some sand in the bottom and made skittles for a bowling game. We collected the lids of old cardboard boxes to use as frames, and with glue and sand and pebbles and seashells and bits of dried seaweed which we found on the beach, the children made lovely collage pictures.

I am telling you all of this because it is important for you to know that in our crèche we don't have money to buy craft materials, we have only the most basic paint and a few old toys, and we have to make most of our things out of scrap materials. We consider ourselves experts at recycling, but the project we were perhaps most proud of was when we found ways to use our sand to make something fun and educational.

So that question you asked me in the first interview, about how good I am at improvising and at solving problems, I think you can see that in Sandveld we have had a lot of practice in solving problems and we are quite good at it sometimes. But the story about how our sand got sold can also tell you how even those things we don't particularly like have some meaning for us, and that we are no different from anyone in the world, we feel connected to the earth even though we have been moved and shunted and relocated a thousand times.

CHAPTER FIVE

I went to my first evening of lectures at university and came back with my head spinning. Mainly it was spinning because I heard so many new ideas and I was so excited about using these ideas in my teaching. But also, my head was spinning because it had been such a long time since I had to study anything, and you really have to focus and concentrate on each word they say, otherwise you can miss something.

Most of my fellow students were at least ten years younger than me, which made me feel a bit weird. I didn't want them to think that I had done nothing all my life and suddenly in middle age realised I wanted to be a teacher, but the lecturer asked each person to introduce himself, and when I told them I had been teaching for twelve years, they were properly respectful!

The course I had signed up for was called 'Cognitive Education'. It is a different kind of teaching from what I learned at Teacher Training College all those years ago. It is quite complicated and it took me months to really understand the difference. I think anything new like that, which means taking something you have been doing for years and doing it in a different way, is quite difficult to learn, because you keep falling back into the old way of doing things and you have to keep on reminding yourself of what is new, and what needs to be done in a different way from before.

I suppose you could say that this kind of teaching, Cognitive Education, has two main things about it. One is *what* we teach the children – and believe me, that was something quite different from what I had always tried to teach. It's not that you shouldn't teach reading and writing and maths, of course you should, but we do it by showing the students how to develop the special thinking skills they need in order to then learn reading and writing and maths. That's the first thing: it is about something more than just learning the usual school subjects. It is about teaching a child how to think, and how to learn.

The second thing which is different in this kind of teaching is *how* we teach. The usual kinds of teaching, which I had been doing all my career, aim to help children learn something, say history for example, and to remember it. If the child doesn't learn it the first time we repeat it again and again. Maybe we try to present the information in different ways, using pictures or asking kids to look it up by themselves.

But in the new kind of teaching, Cognitive Education, just repeating things in different ways is not considered good teaching. I won't go into it all now, I don't want to give you a long lecture on teaching methods, but I'll just give you one example: whatever you teach a child in the classroom, you have to make sure that you make a link, a connection, between that thing and the child's life outside the classroom. So if I am teaching the children to count, it's not enough that they know how to count, they also have to know why counting is so useful in life generally – how your mum counts the amount of money she needs to buy bread, and how we count how many chairs to put in the classroom so every child can sit down, and we have to be very careful to count how many days are in the week otherwise we will go to school on the weekend by mistake.

Maybe that sounds like all you have to do to be a good teacher is to make all the lessons practical, to show the kids how their new knowledge is useful in their lives. But it is more than that. It is showing kids what they did with their minds that helped them to learn this thing, and if they did it once they can do the same kind of thinking again and again to learn other things. We try to teach them to think about their thinking. To be aware of what their minds are doing, instead of being passive receivers of the knowledge we want to hand them.

It's hard to explain. But I think what is special about this way of teaching is that it is a way to help a child *learn how to learn*, instead of just trying to make the children remember more and more information. What I am trying to do with my class now is to give them some skills so that they can learn things on their own, and deal with new information and solve problems, and not just know lots of facts. These days especially, with our kids doing so badly in school, possibly worse than any other country in Africa from what I hear, we need to find a new way to teach.

And in case you think little kids are too young to learn complicated things such as how their thinking works, well you would be surprised what we have managed to achieve with our little four-year-olds.

* * *

One of my assignments for the diploma course was to choose a child in my class I was particularly worried about in relation to his learning, and to describe his difficulties to the class so we could discuss what would be helpful in teaching this child. So of course I chose Devlyn.

We talked a lot, in our tutorials, about what had happened, and was still happening, to children living in poverty and stress and with the kind of losses caused by apartheid. They live in a world which is not organised or systematic. What they see in their world of extreme poverty is a jumble of impressions, feelings, fears and events which seem to occur randomly, without order or reason.

We learned how fear plays a part in whether a child can or cannot learn: that if events and information happen in his world which are random, and not predictable, and each event is dissimilar to what went before, the child will be frightened, or confused, or upset. But if things are made systematic, and he can find a familiar pattern, the child might be calm, and then he might remember what he has learned and be able to build on it.

Well, that made me think immediately of Devlyn, how he didn't seem to do anything systematic, or even do anything for any length of time. He seemed to move randomly from one place to another and from one thing to another. He didn't seem to engage with the world around him in the same way the other children in my class did. Perhaps the events of his life, the randomness of his daily life where he may or may not have had food, or warmth, or safety, or violence and hunger and noise and fear, led to his closing his mind down and instead of listening and learning, he would just keep looking around for danger.

I told the group, and Louise, our lecturer, how sweet and smiling Devlyn was when I spoke to him, but how he would move from one thing to another without stopping, like a butterfly alighting on a flower for seconds before moving on. And how he would not initiate anything, he would not choose a toy, or talk to another child, though he would answer very briefly if I spoke to him. How he seemed not to have learned anything at all in the months he had been in my class, not even to join in with the simple repetitive songs we sang each day.

Some of my classmates suggested he had attention deficit, which would explain why he never settled down to anything, just moved around from one thing to the next. Another person suggested that he might be deaf, had he ever had a hearing test? But Louise said, those things do need to be assessed, you are quite right, but those behaviours you are describing are also typical of a child who has grown up in extreme deprivation and violence. Of course he needs to have a hearing test, of course we must consider attention deficit and also foetal alcohol syndrome, but if we just look at how his life has been until now, we don't really have to wonder why he is like he is.

Instinctively I felt that Devlyn did not have a hearing problem, because he was so alert to the slightest sounds, especially if they seemed to come from the door or window. The sound of footsteps coming towards the classroom alerted him immediately. Even a change in the wind would make him look up, startled.

Louise also reminded us that children can have more than one problem at the same time, and a child who can't hear well can also, at the same time, have attention deficit or learning difficulties, and children will often show all kinds of different behaviours which make it hard for a teacher to know what is going on. It is only through long-term and patient observation, and trying this method and that to help the child, that we can make a hypothesis as to what is stopping this child from learning.

I thought I knew something about what poverty does to people, and especially how it stops children from learning. But Louise made us read article after article about how the actual brain itself is changed by poverty. We read an article about how a state of alarm and stress can lead to a fixed personality trait of hyper-vigilance and constant anxiety; we read how malnutrition and bad housing affects not only the body but also the brain; and we read how parents being absent, either physically or mentally, can affect the way the child's brain develops. Even memory and language are affected by the situations a child finds himself in when living in extreme poverty.

* * *

So all or any of these things could have been what made Devlyn as he was. But what Louise wanted to know from me was, what was I planning to do to help him? A diagnosis is all very well, but maybe it was a luxury we couldn't afford, and maybe it would even distract us from helping Devlyn, because if we accepted that he had a learning difficulty or attention deficit, then what? The risk was that we would use the diagnosis as an excuse to explain why I, Dolores, an experienced teacher, had so far failed to teach him anything.

Well, that set me off I can tell you. There is nothing like a challenge to get me going, especially from a person who is in authority, like a teacher. Or Grandma Rachael.

But where to start?

I was stumped in the beginning, because it's not like I hadn't tried all sorts of things with Devlyn to get him to participate, to do something, anything, for more than a few minutes. But I had to come up with something new because the months were going by and soon he would have to move up to the next class and he certainly wasn't ready for anything like the kind of learning they do with five-year-olds.

One of the things about this teaching method is that in some ways the brain is compared to a computer, and you have to put data into the brain before you can even start thinking about it, remembering it and using that information to solve problems. Louise called it 'input' and I didn't really like that word, I didn't like thinking of children as if they are computers not people, but I got the idea. The child has to get the information from the outside world into his mind, and to do that he needs to look around him, not just at anything but at specific things. And to know what he is looking for, he needs to know what the things in the world are called, the names of all the things he observes. If you don't have the vocabulary, the words, for the world around you, you can't really learn to observe properly because you don't know what you are looking for.

It works both ways. If you don't know how to look around you properly, looking and observing carefully, you won't be able to learn those names, because the world around you will just come and go in a kind of blur, with random events and random scenes, and nothing will make any sense at all. But if you don't know the names, you don't know what to look for. You have to learn how to look, and you have to know what you are looking for, and only then can you use your looking in order to learn.

This is what most babies experience when they are still very tiny: their mother gives them food when they are hungry, she talks to them and notices when they are crying and soothes them. And with this comes words: You're hungry, I know. Here you are, here is your food, here is your mother, oh, look, the sun is shining, you feel better now don't you?

So I had to teach Devlyn those first steps: to look around, to notice things, and to name them.

***

I started to think about all the kinds of words you need to learn if you are a child, just to know something basic about the world you live in. You need words for the space you are in, like big, small, on, under. You need words for the directions you move in, like forwards, backwards, right and left. The world we live in is also a world that is organised in time, not just in space, and learning about time means you have to know words like early, later, tomorrow, yesterday, every Tuesday. And also words like first, next and last. And words like wait, and let's do it again.

I decided that I would stick close to Devlyn, as much as I could during the day considering I still had to teach thirty-five other children, and point out things to him, talk to him regularly, make him notice what was going on around him. Not just the approach of a person towards the classroom, which could signal danger for him, but the daily, ordinary things. Look, the wind is blowing. Look, there is sand all over the floor, let's sweep it up. Look, here are some lovely colours, here is red, here is yellow. It's red like your socks, Devlyn! Come, taste this lovely porridge, this is warm, this is sweet, this is yummy!

So the work I was doing, to put it in the technical terms of Cognitive Education (as I reported it to my classmates a few weeks later in a tutorial with Louise), was to do with helping Devlyn to perceive in a systematic way the world around him, to be aware of what his senses, his eyes and ears, could tell him about his surroundings, and to give all those sensations some meaning. And to give them meaning it would help to label them, to give them names.

And that was the start of his learning. Very, very slowly, so slowly that there were days when I thought nothing would ever change for Devlyn, he started to slow down, to notice things. He would spend a few seconds longer looking at something if I talked to him about it, and would even repeat some of the words I was using to describe what we saw when we were looking at a book or a picture or at the clouds on the mountain which told us rain was coming.

I talked and talked and talked until sometimes I thought I was overdoing it, and certainly some of the kids, Isaac especially, would occasionally look at me strangely. But I saw that Devlyn was listening to me, he was not moving around so much, and that he stopped and listened when I spoke.

I thought it would help Devlyn to keep focused if I kept our classroom routine really systematic and orderly, the same every day, as much as I could, and I noticed how Devlyn started to anticipate things: if we set up the table for food and Bertha was a little delayed in bringing the food, he would look around, and look at me and the table, and look at the door, clearly expecting Bertha. And I would say, yes Devlyn, we are waiting, we are waiting a long time! Where is our food?

I set things up with Bertha so on some days she would deliberately delay bringing the food. So we were all ready, the tables were ready and the children sitting down, and I would say to my class, "Oh dear! We are all ready for food, the table is ready, we are hungry, where is the food?"

And I would send Devlyn with another child to ask Bertha, please can we have some food? Of course Devlyn never spoke, the other child would speak, but he would hear it and see the reaction from Bertha, who always played up to the role: "Oh my goodness! What is the matter with me, I am late! The food! I bring it now-now!" and the two children would come back beaming, with Bertha right behind them carrying the trays of food.

And one glorious day I sent Isaac with Devlyn, and I told Isaac privately not to say anything, but to let Devlyn talk to Bertha, and Bertha told me later that Devlyn had looked straight at her and said, "Bertha, lunch, we hungry!"

Which was the longest sentence I had heard him say, ever.

CHAPTER SIX

Don't think I was spending all my time and energy on Devlyn alone. You can't do that when you have thirty-six lively kids all clamouring for attention and toys and getting into fights and wanting to show you something. So I worked with all of them on learning new words, on observing everything around them and talking about it. And making sure that they didn't just listen to me talking, because I encouraged them to talk too, even the quiet and shy ones.

I tried to encourage them to look around, and to talk about what they could see. What kind of clouds can you see in the sky? What do we expect the weather to be like when we see those clouds? What do we put on the table when we want to eat? And what do we put on the table when we want to cut and glue? What is missing? And we would discuss and talk and learn more and more words.

I started keeping the drawing materials in a cupboard so the kids would have to ask for them. I would sneakily keep back some of the scissors, or the glue sticks, and give out the rest and wait for them to notice what was missing. I wanted them to notice, and to ask specifically for the things they wanted, instead of just passively using whatever I had put on the table.

I asked them to guess what would be for lunch, and to go and search for clues. What is Bertha cooking today? What can you smell? Did you see that man bringing a big bag of rice to the kitchen? So maybe it will be rice! If you look carefully, you will know!

* * *

I also started to teach them vocabulary in categories, or groups, as we had been shown at lectures about the way children learn words. If words are taught in an organised way, by being grouped into categories (for example car, truck and train all belong in the 'transport' group), then children find it easier to remember them. So we talked about weather, and all the words we could use to describe it, and we talked about transport, and stood just inside our school gate noticing and naming every kind of vehicle that went by. I drew pictures of all the kinds of transport we saw, and back in the class we cut them out and arranged them in groups: transport which can carry lots of people (buses and trains), transport which can take only two people (bicycles and motorbikes), transport with engines and transport with no engines (horse-drawn carts).

After a while I had lots and lots of pictures of items from all kinds of categories: food, transport, animals, and sometimes I would mix up all the pictures, put them on a table, and ask the kids seated at that table to sort them out again into groups and to tell me the names of each item.

We always keep in the classroom some items of clothing in a range of different sizes, which we need in case a child wets himself, or comes to school without a warm top or without socks. In this community children often don't have suitable clothing. So I thought I would use those to teach some more vocabulary. For Devlyn it needed to be pretty basic, but for the others I thought I could introduce some more complicated words: we could talk about winter clothes and summer clothes, about creased clothes and ironed clothes, about long- and short-sleeved shirts, and we could look at the patterns on the fabrics, checks or stripes or spots, and compare those to animals which have similar patterns on their coats.

One day I put all our spare clothing in a plastic laundry basket and asked Devlyn, "Are you strong? Can you carry this?" He seemed very happy to prove to me how strong he was and managed to carry the basket, which was nearly as big as he was, to the mat, where the children usually sat while we had a group discussion.

I also borrowed from Bertha in the kitchen a whole lot of cutlery and kitchen implements ("You better bring all this stuff back, hey?! Otherwise how can I cook?!! *Yislaik man,* people are always taking my things!") and I put them in a plastic washing-up bowl and placed those on the mat too. I took one of the old tin cans in which we keep our crayons and paintbrushes and put that on the mat too, having filled it with pencils, some paintbrushes, some crayons, a ruler and scissors. Then I invited the children to sit in a semicircle around me.

I showed the children what we had in the laundry basket: "Look children, here are some clothes. Let's see which clothes we have got here!" and then I offered each child a turn to come and take out one item of clothing, to name it, to say what colour it was, and to decide who could wear this thing. Would it fit a big boy? Or a small girl? Would we wear it when it is cold, in winter, or when it is hot, in summer? We talked about each item, I named each one again, and asked all the children to say the names of the items after me. Then we put them all in a heap on the mat. We did the same thing with the kitchen implements, and then the stationery, putting them on top of the pile of clothing.

I had to keep asking the children to move back, as I kept on dumping things on the mat in the middle of our semicircle, and the pile was getting bigger and bigger and we were running out of space on the mat. They started to giggle each time they had to move again.

"Oh no!" I said in mock despair. "No more space on the mat! What can we do?" and I put even more items on the pile.

"We gotta move, Miss!" they called out in chorus. I sneaked a peek at Devlyn, who was smiling even more broadly than usual but not saying anything.

"Oh!" I repeated. "We need to move, we need to make some space for us to sit. What do we need to do, Devlyn?"

"Move, Miss!" he said, with his lovely smile.

So we moved and moved until by the end of the session we had a huge heap of items jumbled all over the mat and the children were sitting at the edge of the room.

"*En nou*? And now?" I asked the children. "We'd better tidy it all up so we can put the tables out for lunch. Help me, children. Who can bring me some clothes to put in the laundry basket?" and one by one they picked up an item, named it, and put it in the correct container.

And so they learned the names of things, and also the names of each group: 'clothes', 'cutlery', 'stationery'. Some of these words were new to the kids and I could see that, as Louise had told us in our lecture, kids usually pick up the basic names of things much more easily than the group names or category names. The idea behind teaching a category name is that if you know the category name, you will find it easier to learn and remember more names of items which slot into that category. The problem is that category names are hard to learn because they are so abstract. You can't hold up one item and say, "This is a stationery"; you need to show lots of items and show that these are all different *kinds* of stationery.

There were quite a few kids besides Devlyn who didn't know these abstract words. The children who were new to this country, whose first language was neither English nor Afrikaans, certainly needed this kind of work. And even some of the Coloured children, from our community which speaks a mix of English and Afrikaans, didn't know all those words in English.

***

After lunch that day the kids went outside to play. Devlyn was sitting by himself on the bench so I went to sit with him. I pointed to all the clothes he was wearing and asked him to tell me what they were. He managed to name most of them ("Shirt, Miss. Trousers, Miss. Socks, Miss."). Then I asked him, "Is is hot today? Do we need a coat?" pointing to the very blue sky on what was an exceptionally hot day. He looked at me, clearly wanting to answer but not able to. I asked him in Afrikaans and he just looked at me. I tried a different tack, talking in English but asking short, simple questions which needed only a 'yes' or 'no' answer, so Devlyn could show me that he was still listening and understanding what I was saying without having to say very much.

"Whew, it is hot today, *ne*?"

"Yes, Miss."

"Do you want a coat?"

"No, Miss."

"It's too hot for a coat, isn't it, Devlyn?"

"Yes, Miss."

"So will you wear a coat on a hot day?"

"No, Miss."

So he did, after all, understand. Perhaps it was the way I phrased the question ('do we need..?') or perhaps – and this was increasingly the impression I was getting – he was just not used to having a conversation. Maybe that to-and-fro thing that happens in conversation was not something he had experienced. I could easily imagine how that can happen in a family where there is a high level of ongoing stress and poverty and fear: the luxury of having a debate, of having different opinions about something, and taking time to chat about things and consider your options, just isn't there.

So Devlyn could usually answer if I asked him a specific question, and in our activity with the clothes and the kitchen utensils he knew exactly which item belonged in which group, but when it came to saying anything other than in response to a question he was silent. Quiet, but not still – he was always in motion, moving, looking around him.

***

The next day Devlyn was not at school. I popped over to Sophie at the Shebeen to ask if his mother had been in and she told me she hadn't seen her. Perhaps Devlyn or the baby was ill. But the day after that Devlyn again didn't come to school. He was always such a regular attender, in fact of all the children in my class, he was one of the few who had not missed a single day since he started school. So I was quite worried, and after talking to Frances, we looked up his address in the file.

Bertha called her husband, who was as usual hanging around the school, trying to find something useful to do. Since he had lost his job as a gardener he had been unemployed, and while we loved having him around (there was nothing he could not fix), we knew he desperately needed a job – if only to keep his beloved car going.

Martinus' car was a miracle, because even though it had four wheels and a roof, it didn't really have a floor, and when we drove in it we could see the road going by underneath us and we had to keep our feet carefully balanced on a plank he had installed. Also there was no reverse gear so he could only go forward, which made it very hard to park. If someone parked in front of him, he had to wait until they moved before he could get out of the parking space.

We drove to Overcome Heights, where Devlyn lived. It is a very short drive from our school, in fact it is not even a separate township, just some shacks on the empty stretch of sand with Sandveld on one side and Lilac Hill, the next town, on the other.

I had only been there once before when I was on my way in a taxi to Lilac Hill and the driver told me he knew a short cut via Overcome, and to tell you the truth I hoped I wouldn't have to go there ever again. There are no roads, just paths between the shacks, so Martinus parked the car in the open field and we hoped it would be there when we got back. We kind of joked that it was the perfect parking place for Martinus' car because there were no other cars around to park him in, but actually we weren't feeling so happy or jokey because we were so worried about Devlyn and what we would find.

To get to a home in Overcome you have to walk between the shacks, and there are no street signs. All the paths are usually muddy because there is no piped water so people have to get their bucket of water from the one tap and walk with the water sloshing over the sides of the bucket, back to their house. After they have cooked or washed the dishes, the dirty water is just thrown outside their house. There are plastic bags and litter lying all over, and the wind doesn't help: if anyone ever thinks they can tidy up by putting all the garbage in one place, the wind will make sure it is spread out evenly all over.

I had been talking with my class about using your senses to get information, and here my senses were assaulted in every way. Everything in this place looked broken. What I could smell was raw sewage. What I could hear was a baby crying.

Overcome Heights. What an ironic name. To think I had been teaching Devlyn vocabulary, that things have names and that their names help us make sense of the world, and he was living in a place called Overcome, which makes no sense whatsoever. How is it possible to overcome this? Maybe it means, when you go there, you are overcome. With meaninglessness and senselessness.

There were a few people walking around and some just sitting down outside their shacks, and we asked them if they knew where Devlyn and his mother lived. Finally we were directed to a shack. We knocked on the door. There was no answer but we could hear a baby crying inside. So we pushed open the door, it wasn't locked, and we were hit by the stench of faeces and the darkness and we could see through the dark that there was a baby lying on the floor crying and there was Devlyn, this time not smiling, just trying to pat the baby, to do something, but he didn't know what to do and anyway he was only four, he was a baby himself.

It wasn't even a shack, just a few pieces of corrugated iron leaning on each other, with the wind blowing in between the gaps. The floor had some bits of lino over the earth but it was damp and filthy.

We didn't know what to do. Surely their mother was somewhere nearby? We said hello to Devlyn, I hugged him and Frances picked up the baby; Martinus looked around outside the shack, but we saw nobody. We couldn't leave them like that, the baby needed a clean nappy and some food and Devlyn needed... what did he need? He needed a safe house, a place with a mother who would take care of him, he needed not to be responsible at age four for a baby. So I picked up Devlyn – he was so tiny, so light, he weighed nothing at all – and we went to the next shack to tell them that if the kids' mother came back they should tell her that the children were fine, we were taking them to Sunbeams nursery, and we left. Our car was still there, Martinus luckily managed to start it the first time, and we bundled the kids in and drove back to Sunbeams.

I was shaking. Did we do wrong? Who knew how long they had been there alone? Who knew what had happened to their mother and whether she was ever coming back, or even alive?

Frances took the baby home and washed her and dressed her in clean clothes and gave her a bottle of milk, and phoned Lorraine, who is a Trustee, and she came over immediately to hear about what had happened. Lorraine decided to phone the police. I wish it could have been social services that we phoned, but there are no local social services here and the regional phone number just rang and rang. So it had to be the police. Usually we only phone the police if there is big violence in the streets, because they can't do anything to help us when we are in this kind of trouble, but who else could we phone?

We didn't know if the kids had eaten anything since we last saw them two days ago, never mind what else could have happened while they were there in that shack all alone. I asked Bertha to stay with Devlyn and to give him something to eat and drink and I went back to my class and we tried to get back into the normal day's learning routine, although I was shaken by the thought of Devlyn (not to mention that baby!) living in those squalid conditions, perhaps starving, certainly cold and dirty, and being so totally unprotected, unsafe, with no adult around.

Bertha popped around to Sophie at the Shebeen to tell her that if Devlyn's mother came by, she should tell her the kids were safe with us.

That night Devlyn and the baby slept at Frances' house. Frances is so used to taking in stray children for a night or two that she has mattresses and blankets ready, folded under her bed, and we collected some nappies and took some clothes for Devlyn to wear from the collection which ironically, in our class just a few days before, we had been sorting and naming to teach vocabulary.

CHAPTER SEVEN

Annetjie, Devlyn's mother, appeared the next day. She had a black eye and she looked dazed. It turned out (Sophie at the Shebeen knew everything) that Annetjie had, a few years ago, been in a relationship with a gang member, and a rival gang now wanted to send him a warning but couldn't find him. So instead they had kidnapped her, just for a day or two, to teach him a lesson.

It is nothing unusual for a woman to be beaten or abused in Sandveld. An officer from the police had come to speak to us the previous year at the school to tell us (which was nothing we didn't already know) that in Sandveld they are called out about thirty times a month, that means on average at least once every single day, for domestic violence complaints. He said it is worse here than in neighbouring areas because people live in such crowded housing, there is so much alcohol and drugs, and people don't have jobs. He said that Shebeens are also the problem, because they serve alcohol and some people get drunk and violent, but when I think of Sophie I only see her shepherding her kids after school and it is hard to see how she could be the cause of any kind of problem.

The saddest thing the policeman told us is that some women, mothers, are being beaten by their own sons, to get money for drugs. When I asked the policeman why he was telling us all this, he said, "We think it may be helpful if you could teach kids at school that they have rights, that they can say no to abuse, and if their mother is in trouble they should tell someone at the school, and maybe get help. We can't be inside the houses, we can't see what is happening, and we only find out about it afterwards. So we rely on women and children to keep us informed, and sometimes we can help."

I thought it strange that the police need the weakest people in society, the women and children, to help them, while the strongest people get away (sometimes literally) with murder. Well, that's how it is here.

When Annetjie came back she was so confused she couldn't tell Sophie what had really happened, and she just kept asking, "My kids, are they okay? My kids?" Frances took Annetjie and the kids to spend a second night in her house, and the next day Lorraine from the Trust called everyone she knew and suddenly there was a room made available in a small house not far from the library in Sandveld. So it meant they would get out of Overcome Heights and live in a proper room, with a window, and a door that closes, and a roof that doesn't leak, and with other people living in the house so they wouldn't be alone and afraid.

***

I want to tell you about the first time I noticed that something was wrong, or maybe something was missing, in the way I was teaching.

A regular part of every school day here at Sunbeams is drawing. We have crayons which we put in empty baked bean tins in the middle of the table, and we have big sheets of paper. The paper is donated to us by a business in the industrial park on the edge of our township. The man who owns that business sometimes comes to visit us, he wants to be a good neighbour to us he says, and he often brings us stationery and other supplies. He also gives us their used paper, which has lots of computer stuff on one side but the other side is blank, and when we thank him he says that anyway he would just throw it away if he didn't give it to us.

I used to think my four-year-olds were drawing nicely, and that it was a good enough thing for them to practise holding a pencil or a crayon and just seeing what would happen when they made marks on a page. They didn't seem to be drawing anything specific; you couldn't say, "This is a picture of a such-and-such", and when I asked them what they had drawn, they usually couldn't tell me. They seemed to enjoy doing it but it was hard to tell, maybe it was just part of classroom routine and they knew they were supposed to do it, but I never once had a child come up to me and show me what he had drawn.

It worried me that when we gave out all the drawings to the kids at the end of each day, no child ever recognised his own drawing, so if their name had not been written on it we just handed out any drawing so each child would have one to take home. It was as if they hadn't looked at what they were drawing while they were doing it, and hadn't connected themselves to it in a way which would make them say, "I did that. It's mine."

It didn't bother me until I started visiting Silverleaf School, and sat in the classroom with their four-year-olds, the same age as my kids. I was astounded. Even when a drawing was nothing any adult could identify, the child could always say, this is a ship, and this is a man, and here is the sea. They knew what they could see in their mind and they knew what they had put on the paper. And at the end of a day, the teacher would hold up each drawing and say, whose picture is this? And each child would recognise his own picture and stand up and say, that is mine.

I couldn't stop thinking about the difference between my kids and the Silverleaf kids. What was going on? It couldn't be that all the Silverleaf children were simply born artists and would all grow up to be gifted at art. If that was the case, there would be a special museum for all the famous artists who graduated from that school.

I went back to my class the next day, put out the materials and just sat and watched. And what I saw was this: the kids were having a good time. They were drawing. But they were also spending a lot of time talking to each other, and while they were talking they were still drawing but they didn't look at their pictures. Some of them managed to finish a picture, to draw quite a lot of marks on the page, without having looked at their page for more than a few seconds. I saw Devlyn take a crayon without even looking what colour it was, and once I noticed that, I realised that quite a lot of the kids just stretched out their hand and took whatever came to hand, and made marks and didn't look at the effect their hand and their crayon had had on the page. No wonder they didn't recognise their own drawings. They hadn't been looking when they drew them.

How could this be? I knew our kids had nothing wrong with their vision, because we have their eyes tested once every year; someone comes from the local optician. She volunteers one day each year, and she tests every single child. We have the same for hearing tests: a volunteer comes from the big hospital, they set up a quiet space (not easy here!) and they check every single child's hearing. It is something that the Trust arranged when Sunbeams was set up, right from the beginning. So if they could see, why didn't they look?

That's when I started to understand what the lecturer at university had been telling us about looking and about input: that maybe learning to look is not something a baby does automatically, like sucking, or learning to stand and walk. Maybe it is a different thing, something you have to actually teach a baby. And I know how the parents of my kids live. They get up before the sun rises, make sure that everyone has something to eat (if there is any food in the house), try to get themselves and the kids washed using the one bucket of water they filled last night, find everyone's clothes even though there is no place to store things properly and maybe only one wardrobe in the entire house, get everyone out of the house in time, get the kids to school or to Sophie at the Shebeen, get to the bus stop and hope to get a place on one of the crowded taxis or buses, work all day, and then reverse the whole trip at the end of a day. During the day something would have happened at the taxi rank or in the township, someone would have been arrested or shot, there may or may not be enough food for everyone for dinner, and the roof may be leaking again. When is such a parent to find time to say to her child, "Look! Look at the lovely sunset, look at the flowers, aren't they lovely? Aren't the colours beautiful?" and these kids certainly didn't have books, and some of their parents couldn't even read, so it would never be that these parents could have the time or the space or the equipment to say, "Look, look at this picture, what do you think the child is doing here?"

Stopping to look at things, and to describe them, is such a luxury in life. In Sandveld, what you need to look at, or look for, is a leaking ceiling, and did your kid get home safely from school without being attacked on the way, and how to divide a chicken leg into four pieces.

That was when I started to feel that I now had a different kind of responsibility at Sunbeams. I was the one who was chosen to go and get special training at Silverleaf School and at university. And the teachers were starting to ask me how to do things, how to teach a child who just can't learn, and what they could do differently to improve things. And I was starting to see the problem of how to teach our kids in a whole different light.

But still I hesitated. Maybe I was wrong. Maybe our kids didn't have a problem with looking. Maybe I was just getting excited about nothing.

It wouldn't be the first time that had happened.

I wanted to be sure that my theory about looking in order to learn was correct before I started talking to the other teachers at Sunbeams about this new idea of mine. I needed to be sure that the kids I had in my class really didn't know how to look at something and describe it accurately.

So I spoke to Louise at university, and I asked her how she would find out if a child really did have this kind of problem, how she would test for it. She told me about a test which she used; you had to buy an expensive kit and get the training to use it, and it was only for use by psychologists not teachers, but she said one of the things that test asks children to do is to look at a picture where there is lots going on, lots of people doing different things, and then you ask them to describe the picture. And then you write down exactly what they say, and how long their sentences are, and what they notice, and how they use their words and their language to describe it to you. And from their answers you can get a good idea about their language development as well as about their ability to observe details and make sense of a picture.

So I said to myself, well, Dolores, this is your job! You are their teacher, you have all day at school, get going now!

I chose five kids for my little research project. Two were the oldest in my class; they were confident and talkative and always seemed to understand what I was saying and to respond to it appropriately. They could speak English and Afrikaans, and they were very popular in the class and everyone wanted to play with them.

The next two were kids who were having problems with some of the classroom activities: they couldn't do puzzles, and they didn't really join in the singing. They were also a bit younger than most of the others, but they were making progress and taking part in the day's activities more and more.

And the fifth child was Devlyn.

Patricia, the librarian at the Sandveld library, suggested some picture books, and I chose a busy, brightly coloured picture where there was lots of activity and lots to talk about, but which also looked a bit like Sandveld itself. Because, believe me, most of the picture books show a world which is totally unrecognisable to a child who has never left Sandveld. Most of them show huge double-storey brick houses with big windows and red-tiled roofs and trees and gardens, and a big shiny car in a garage, and they show children playing with wonderful toys like Lego and shiny toy cars. Or they show forests with hundreds of trees, while here in Sandveld I think the whole town has maybe three trees.

So I had to be sure my kids wouldn't fall silent just from sheer amazement at the kinds of things in those pictures, things they had never seen in their lives.

I sat with each of these five children in turn, and I asked each child to tell me what he could see in the picture.

I carefully wrote down every word they said. One of the two older and more sociable kids told me, "Boy playing with a ball, cars driving." I said, "What else?" He said, "Trucks driving." I said, "What else?" He said, "Another boy playing."

I had to work hard to draw him out, to point and hint and persuade, to get more of a description. And this was a boy who was competent, sociable, confident and talkative! But it seemed he just had no experience of looking at a picture, in a book, and talking about it. Looking and describing, one of the most important things you need to do at school, was simply something he had never been asked to do.

Imagine having to write a report at school about the results of a science experiment, or evaluating a painting, without being able to look and describe.

The two kids in my 'middle ability' group were, not surprisingly, even worse. They did look, but briefly, and they said one or two words, but they just named single things when I pointed to them, and didn't offer any of their own ideas. And they didn't produce even one single sentence; it was single words only. So it was a very one-sided kind of conversation, where I asked "What is this?", and if they knew the word they answered me, and if they didn't they said nothing.

When it was Devlyn's turn, he just looked at the picture briefly, then looked at me, and smiled. I asked him to look again, I pointed to the child, the car, the truck, the birds. He pointed too, and said nothing.

Well, I thought, maybe these kids haven't had enough experience with a task like this. In fact, I felt a bit guilty, because I do read them stories from picture books every day, and I do show them the pictures while I read to them, and so do all the other teachers at Sunbeams, but mostly I talk and they listen to me talking. I hadn't really encouraged the kids themselves to talk.

Oops. I could just hear Louise saying, if you want a child to talk, give him chances to talk! You need to encourage them, to set the situation up so that they will feel that talking is a good thing to do. That is what teaching is about, setting up situations so that kids can do what they are nearly, nearly ready to do but just can't get there on their own, without you helping them to take the next little step.

That is such a big part in Cognitive Education. It is about thinking what the next step could be for a child, and making it possible for the child to take that next step. Louise called it 'scaffolding' and other people called it fancy names like 'zone of development', but actually it is just about showing the child where that next step is and making it possible for him to take it.

So I went back and I tried something different to help my kids to look carefully and notice things, even if they could not talk about it. I cut a longish thin rectangle out of cardboard and stuck two little square pieces of coloured paper on it: on the left a little red square, and next to it, on its right, a little blue square. Then I took a blank rectangle of cardboard the same size and placed some coloured paper squares on the table and asked the five children to copy what I had done, to stick two squares, the same colour, on their cardboard so it would look the same as mine.

Well, that may sound simple to you, but they couldn't do it. They didn't have a sense of the pattern or the sequence of it, and they needed me to tell them what to look at, and where to stick the pieces, and which one went where. Once I had shown them a few examples, the older, more advanced children caught on, but the middle group just didn't get it.

At our next tutorial, when I reported back to Louise and my tutorial group about how my little experiment had gone, we all agreed that being able to do this task was not only about looking and observing in detail but also about understanding pattern and sequence: things which are really important in lots of areas in school but especially in maths. Louise also wanted us to be clear that this seemingly very simple task of matching (this is a blue square, find another one exactly the same, find me another blue square) is not something which a child grows up to do naturally but which has to be taught explicitly. So I added matching and sequencing to the activities I did with Devlyn.

* * *

A few of the younger children started to be interested in what I was doing with Devlyn. They started gathering around us as soon as they saw me sitting down with him. Maybe it was the individual attention, which every child (and adult!) craves. But that turned out to be a useful thing: they got involved in the activities, they started to ask for materials to work with, and soon I had a little group of children who were beginning to make sense of the world around them, learning to name things and to describe things. I collected examples of everything they did in a big folder and took it to Louise each week to report back on how my kids, and I, were learning about Cognitive Education.

It was lovely that the kids were enjoying the activities, and clamouring for more, but I think I was even more excited than they were about it.

CHAPTER EIGHT

I was aware that I was teaching a kind of programme which was not the norm in our kind of school, and I wanted to make sure that I wasn't expecting something from my class which they were simply too young to be able to do. So the next Wednesday when I went off to Silverleaf for my observation day, I took the picture book with me that I had asked my kids to describe and also some of my cardboard rectangles and coloured squares, and I asked the teacher of the four-year-olds if I could sit with a few of their children, some of the youngest, the most quiet children, and look at the book. I sat with a little boy who initially didn't feel comfortable sitting with a total stranger, but his teacher sat with us too, so he relaxed.

I opened the page. "What can you see?" He started out quietly, almost in a whisper, but gradually the words started coming out of his mouth. "It's a boy, he's playing with a ball, and here is a cement truck, taking the cement to the building, they are building a new house, and the car is going on the road. And there is a dog, he is sitting here. And here are birds flying, flying in the sky, and here is the mountain, and the sun."

Then I did the exercise with the little coloured squares, and after I explained it to him only once, he could copy my patterns easily. Not just two squares, but three and even four squares in a row.

I was stunned at the difference between this child and my two most competent four-year-olds. How come this young child, known to be struggling to keep up with the rest of his class, was so good at looking and describing? Was it that our kids didn't have enough language to describe what they saw, or was it that they just didn't know how to look? And, of course, most of our children have no books at home, they can't afford them, and so many of our children's parents can't read because education for non-White people has been such a disaster in this country over so many generations, so our children just haven't had the experience that other children have had.

Maybe it was all of those things. I told the teacher who was sitting with me about my idea of creating a special programme to help my kids to learn to look and observe, and she was very interested in it all, until I said, "I think my kids need to be taught how to draw."

She didn't like the idea. "We never teach our kids to draw. Art sessions are time for them to do whatever is in their heads. It is their creative time, we never ever interfere in what they want to draw. We teach lots of things, letters and sounds, and numbers, and songs, and behaviour, but we definitely don't teach drawing!"

***

At the end of that school day at Silverleaf, when the parents were picking up their kids, I lingered at the door to watch them. Each child came out of the class holding his drawings of the day, and some of the parents sat down on the step or stopped walking and bent down to look at their child's pictures, and I could see they were pointing and looking carefully and talking about what they saw.

One of the mums, who was standing outside the building waiting for her child to come out of the classroom, was holding her six-month-old baby in her arms and she was saying to her, "Look! Just look at the mountain! It's huge, isn't it?"

Silverleaf School is built right at the foot of the almost vertical Table Mountain, which loomed over us, a giant friendly presence. The cloud cover was coming down and this mother just kept on looking, and kept on talking about it to her child and pointing, "Look: it's the tablecloth! It's coming down over the mountain." And all the children coming out of the classroom were looking up and watching the tablecloth coming down.

And her baby was looking, following her pointing finger.

* * *

Learning to look. I understood now that parents who are not poor, or rushed, who are not worried or hungry or exhausted, have the time to stop and look, and can show their kids how to do that.

So I decided. Worrying about limiting my kids' creativity by teaching them to draw was not the point. It would be much, much worse to do nothing, not to intervene, to just accept this state my kids were in.

Teaching them to look, to observe the world around them accurately instead of letting things impinge randomly on their awareness, seemed to me something I had a duty to do, and something my kids had a right to be taught, just like any other child. And drawing would be just one of the ways I would do it. "Enough agonising, Dolores!" I said to myself. "You have a job to do."

'Learning to look and looking to learn'. That was what I called the new programme.

* * *

I started the very next day. I asked Bertha to give me five oranges which she was going to serve later as the mid-morning snack. She was a bit reluctant. "Make sure you bring them back, *hey*. We only got just enough oranges today, half an orange for each child!" I promised solemnly to bring them back.

Then I realised we didn't actually have a full range of colours in each tin. Only two of the five tins had an orange crayon. I asked Isaac to run to all the other classrooms and ask the teachers for all the orange crayons they had. "And tell them we will bring them back," I said.

Resources are in scarce supply here in Sandveld.

I asked the children to sit in a circle around me and held up one of the oranges. "Who can tell me the name of this colour?" I asked. Many of the kids, and Isaac of course, knew the colour, but the foreign children, and Devlyn too, sat quietly.

"Orange!" I said. And I held up lots of things that were orange, which I had collected and put in a plastic bag. Orange trousers. Orange scarf. Orange flower. Orange mug. I had even found, in the pile of throwaway stuff at Silverleaf School the day before, some orange wrapping paper and I smoothed it out and held it up.

Then I took one of the crayon tins and started taking out one colour at a time.

"Is this orange?" I asked, holding up a blue crayon.

"NO!" they chorused.

"Is this orange?" I held up a red crayon.

"NO!"

"Is this orange?"

"Yes!"

I held up the oranges and said to the kids, "Look! These are oranges, their name is orange and their colour is orange! And later, Bertha is going to cut these up and each person will eat half an orange. Can you see this colour? It's the same as this crayon. Orange!"

Now we were ready. The children sat at their tables to draw. I put the orange crayons in the crayon tins among the other colours. Then I asked the children to look carefully in their crayon tins, to take only the orange colour, and to draw with it. At this stage I didn't mind what they drew, I just wanted them to think about a specific colour, to look for it, to actively search for and choose one colour. At the end, I held up each picture, all thirty of them, and talked about the colour they had used, and the shapes and lines they had drawn, and we speculated together what each child had drawn. I made sure all of them had a good look at each picture, and afterwards I gave them each a high-five for being so good at looking at the pictures.

You are probably amazed. You are probably thinking, surely this kind of activity is more suited to children who are only two or three years old? Yes. That is true. But our kids have come from a different past from yours, and what they have lost in the past generations is still missing for them, and I have to give it back to them.

I asked Devlyn and another child to take the oranges back to Bertha, and when she later brought them to us, cut in half, for our snack, it was lovely to see how excited the children were. We actually have oranges as a snack quite often when they are in season, they are cheap here, so it was nothing new, but suddenly it seemed that there was a kind of recognition, as if they were looking at something they had never seen before.

* * *

Sometimes when I tell people about the project, at first they don't believe me. "Surely, if a child can see, if his eyes are okay, he can look?" they say.

I still have to explain to these people, over and over, because it is hard to understand, what it is like in poverty, how focused looking and noticing are not necessarily things every baby does automatically. They breathe, they suck, they lift up their heads, they crawl. But this is something different, something you have to show them how to do.

"Come and look for yourselves!" I would say, "Come one day and watch my kids." But nobody came to visit us and I just carried on with my programme.

CHAPTER NINE

I had hoped we could have some calm time after all that trouble with Annetjie, and just focus on learning and playing, but no. About a week later we started an epidemic of stomach flu at the nursery. It's always like that: one child gets ill and they all catch it from him.

But many children still come to school when they are sick because their parents don't dare take time off work for a sick child. So even though we have a school rule that says please don't send a sick child to school, we know very well, and the parents know too, that we won't send anyone home because they will be at home by themselves, and that is not safe. So we set up a corner of Frances' office with a mattress and blankets, and kids who were sick could go and lie down and nap there under her eye.

We set up a rota of teachers to take kids to the toilet or to hold their heads while they were being sick, but it was always hard because there is only one teacher in each class and you can't leave a class full of children alone. We tried to get someone, either Bertha or Frances, to come and sit in the class while we did our rota but it was a hard time, every few hours another kid getting ill.

Then the teachers started catching it. We phoned the Trust and double quick they arranged for two substitute teachers to come in while two of our teachers were off sick.

One of the teachers of the youngest group, Ruth, was first to be ill and she came back to school two days later looking exhausted but determined that she was now okay and fully recovered. But when the kids were out in the playground I went up to her to see how she was. She sat down on the paving stones. "I am just so tired, you know? But it's fine, it's over now."

And then she told me, "You know what is the hardest thing about this sickness? I live in a backyard shack, behind a house, I don't have a toilet. So I have to wait all night to go to the toilet, they only let me in to the house at 5.30 when they get up to go to work. That is the hardest thing."

I have to explain for those of you who don't know how things are here in South Africa. Some people live in a small house and in their back yard they put up shacks, nothing special, not big, just a corrugated iron roof and some walls and a door. Lots of people need to live close to town so that they can get to work, and if they can't afford a house they live in these backyard shacks. Ruth is one of these. She came to Cape Town from the Eastern Cape a few years ago when her husband died. Her children are with her mother in the Eastern Cape and she works here as a teacher and sends them money. And she lives with no toilet. She said to me, "I am lucky, I know lots of people who have to use the bucket toilets, one toilet for every twenty families, and it is dangerous to go there at night so they are waiting all night to go, and when they do get there, it is filthy, stinking, people don't know how to behave. So at least I have got a clean toilet, a proper toilet and a shower and a sink. But not at night, and it was at night I needed it when I was sick. So, whew! Thank goodness,

I am better now!" and with that she got up and called her kids to come back into class.

So it was a hard week. Cleaning up after so many sick kids, and then rushing back to class only to find another one was sick, made me wonder what kind of person would take on a job like this.

* * *

And then after work when I got to the taxi rank to get home, I could see that something had happened. People were huddled together, talking, gesticulating. I asked someone what was going on. "There was a shooting at a taxi rank up the road, in Steenberg. One driver is dead, two passengers are hurt."

Again I have to explain if you don't know how our transport system works. Most of us Blacks and Coloureds don't have cars. So we take a bus or a train or a minibus taxi to get to work. The bus routes only go on the main roads and there aren't that many buses anyway, so most of us travel by taxi.

The taxi I am talking about is not the kind of taxi where you have one passenger and one driver. The driver waits till there are enough people to fill his taxi and he doesn't like to go until it is full. He has an assistant who sits with him and calls out the destination in a loud voice, and he jumps in and out the taxi at each stop to try to attract some more passengers so the taxi will always be full of people. The driver stops to let people out wherever they need to get off and then picks up more people along the route if they wave to him, so it's a bit informal, there isn't a timetable or anything, you just wait till a taxi comes and get a seat if you can.

On that day, there were very few drivers around, maybe they were scared off by the shooting, which is usually the result of turf warfare among taxi drivers. So by the time I got a seat on a taxi it was already getting dark. I knew Johannes would be worried about me but I didn't have airtime on my phone so I just sat there. The taxi was full to bursting and I could hardly breathe, people were sitting so close to me with their parcels and their bags and some of them not so thin either.

So you can imagine I was quite pleased to get home and Johannes had already eaten at work and had made dinner for me and Elise, so I didn't have to cook. I was going to tell him about the taxi ride and about Ruth and then I remembered Overcome Heights and I thought, Grandma Rachael, your words come back to me these days more and more. "*My kind*, my child, remember, there is always someone worse off than you, so stop your talking, get your homework done and come and help me prepare dinner." So I just washed my hands and sat down with Elise to eat.

* * *

I think I already told you that idea from Cognitive Education that if you only teach school subjects, and if you think that education is only about school, you are not doing your job properly. A teacher has to make sure the children can apply what they have learned in class to their lives outside school.

Well, the teachers have to do the same for themselves: they have to learn to live with that kind of thinking, not just while doing their job but in their daily lives too. Some people feel that it is really a kind of philosophy, this thing, it is a way you start thinking, and once you start it takes over completely. But I wasn't there yet, it was all too new and different for me and I still kept it firmly inside the boundaries of what I did at work.

So while I was trying to teach my class to look, and to notice, I didn't realise that I wasn't applying those new ideas to myself at all. I myself had stopped looking at anything other than what I was doing at school.

So I didn't notice that our street, Seagull Street where Sunbeams school is, was not looking so good these days. It's a funny thing, when you are surrounded by something every day, year after year, you stop noticing. Or maybe, you can be very good at looking at what is interesting, and what makes you feel good, like how I could be a better teacher, but you don't look at what is horrible and ugly, and so I just didn't even see that our street was filthy. It was easier not to look and not to see.

I am sure if you ever visit Sandveld you will see that we don't have many tarred roads, it is mainly dirt roads with potholes and puddles. In spite of that, some of our streets are really quite clean, and there is no rubbish on the side of the road, because the people who live in those streets make sure to keep it clean: they never throw rubbish on the ground, and if they see someone else throw something they pick it up. Of course, the wind makes it almost impossible to keep clean because the minute you have picked up some rubbish the wind will send you some more. But some streets are more or less okay.

But some other streets, where there are lots of people who are renting a room for a few days and who don't care about the town, are a real mess, and our street, Seagull Street, is sometimes not something to be proud of, I admit it. So what I did was this. I decided we would have a special project, to try to clean up our street.

I planned it with Frances, because we had to get the parents' permission to take the kids up and down the road during school hours.

The other precaution we had to take was to warn the children to be really careful not to pick up anything dangerous. It's really sad, but here in Sandveld, and not only here, in lots of poor areas, people are using drugs and they sometimes throw their syringes on the ground. Also lots of drinking goes on and bottles get broken and there can be glass on the road. So I spent a lot of time talking to the children before the clean-up day, showing them pieces of glass and pictures of children who had cut their hands and were bleeding, and making sure they would know not to pick up glass. The local doctor gave us a few discarded syringes, without the needles, and I brought needles from my sewing kit, and I showed the children never, never, never to touch anything like this.

And to make sure that they knew what I meant, that there were some things they must never touch, I reminded them about rules that they already knew: that we never touch the electrical outlets in the wall, and we never touch a fire, that's a rule, and we never pick up glass or a syringe or a needle. Only paper and Coke tins!! It's a rule, just like waiting your turn to get on the slide, and not taking two pieces of orange when there is only one for each child. Those are rules too.

I also managed to sneak in a few words about looking carefully, because if you pick up some rubbish and just throw it any old how towards the person holding the bin bag, the paper will fall right out. But if you look, and make sure the paper goes right inside the bag, then it will stay there. Just like when you put your foot in your shoe and it has to go exactly in the right place, otherwise your shoe will fall off.

We waited for a fine day, when it wasn't blowing too hard, and we all lined up, Frances and my children and me. Every third child had a black garbage bag, because they are quite expensive, so the first thing was to decide who held the bags, and believe me that wasn't easy because they all wanted to have a bag.

There was a bit of shoving and shouting, and some sulky faces, but eventually I decided to give each child a number from one to three, which I pinned on his shirt. A third of the class were Ones, another third were Twos, and the rest were Threes. I explained to them that the numbers matter, because first all the Ones would hold a bag and the others would fill the bags, but then I would blow my whistle and the Ones would give their bag to a Two, and later, after another whistle, a child with a Three would get the bag.

That way every single child got a chance to hold a bag, it was fair, nobody got left out, and all because we had numbers to help us! So I could point out to them that numbers are really helpful, that is why we need to learn to count, and that is why we need to be able to recognise the numbers, otherwise how would we know which child is a One or a Two or a Three?

* * *

Well, you can imagine that with all the preparation and all the explaining, the kids were just raring to go, and in fact we had a lovely hour's activity and the road looked so much better afterwards. Lorraine from the

Trust, mindful of publicity as ever, had leaked our plan to a photographer from the local newspaper and he came along and took photos which were in the paper two days later. I don't need to tell you how proud my children were, to see themselves in a newspaper.

And true to the principles of Cognitive Education, where you talk to children about what they have done, and try to make them aware of the links between actions and the thoughts behind them, and teach them how planning things makes them go well, I spent time after we got back to our class talking to them about all the wonderful things they had achieved: looking carefully to find the rubbish and putting it carefully inside the bags, and making everything look nice, and also their good behaviour in agreeing to take turns, and following the rules, and how they used the numbers to make sure it was fair and each child got a turn to hold a bag. I gave them heaps of praise, not just for cleaning the street, which was wonderful in itself, but for all these things they had learned and done.

And I was really starting to feel that now I understood this Cognitive Education thing. It is a lot more than teaching subjects at school. My kids were learning to look around them, to really see what there was to see, and to make sensible decisions about what you can do once you can really see, instead of just sitting passively waiting for someone else to clean up for you, or for your teacher to give you pencils or glue or lunch. I started to see more of them taking books from the shelf and really spending time looking at them, turning pages much more slowly now because they were taking in information in a quite different way. And I was involving them more and more in planning our games and activities, to show them how you first think about things and then do them.

* * *

I had not forgotten the response I got from the teachers at Silverleaf about my ideas for teaching drawing. To tell the truth, I was irritated by it, and I shouldn't have been, because I think they just didn't know how our kids' lives are so different from their kids' lives. I always say if you haven't lived in South Africa for a while, you can't even begin to imagine what it is like, and in the same way, if you haven't lived in a place like Sandveld, you can't have even the faintest idea of what it is like for our kids.

But I was also cross with myself, because instead of explaining my ideas to them, and telling them why it seemed important, I just stayed silent when I heard their reaction. I just couldn't think what to say, and why my idea, which had seemed so simple and so sensible, suddenly seemed like something which was wrong from an educational point of view but also, somehow, and this was even worse, wrong from a moral point of view.

What I should have said to those teachers was that they perhaps didn't realise that looking is not something a child learns automatically, just by growing and by having eyes to see. Seeing may be something that just happens, it is a fact of biology, but seeing is not the same as looking, and hearing is not the same as listening.

I didn't tell them what I had observed when I watched mothers of Silverleaf kids talking to their children and telling them, look, look at that, let's look for this. For goodness sake, these teachers were doing it all day long without even knowing they were doing it. Look at this picture in the book, what do you think will happen next? Look at this lovely new tablecloth we have on our table! Look at the wonderful tower that Johnny built, isn't it tall?

My reputation at home, when I was a child, had always been as the person who never stopped arguing until someone listened and agreed with me. 'Dolores the nag' I was called, and don't think I didn't see when my uncles would roll their eyes when I tried to tell them what they should be doing. Of course Grandma Rachael also called me the dreamer, which seems like a contradiction: how can you be nagging if you are dreaming? But it makes sense to me: when I was dreaming, it was usually about how to persuade people to do what I wanted them to. It was about how to get them to see what I saw, to see my point of view about something important.

Though maybe sometimes I was trying to dream up something new to nag about, just for practice.

But somehow, when I was at Silverleaf nursery, I fell silent. I didn't nag and in fact I would actually find myself forgetting what it was I had felt so strongly about the day before, at Sunbeams, and which I had looked forward to talking about with the Silverleaf teachers. And that is not like me, I am usually a bit too outspoken for my own good, so I didn't understand what was happening to me.

Frances was too diplomatic to say it, but Patricia, my friend the librarian, doesn't mince words, and she said to me straight out: "Dolores, you are intimidated by those people because they are White!"

After the initial shock of hearing what Patricia said, I did stop and think. How many times had I heard

Grandma and the uncles debating what they should have done about the forced removals? Should they have spoken out, should they have argued, or should they have tried to be more polite? How polite did they need to be when the White municipal inspectors came into people's houses to look around, and make notes, and to tell them they would have to move? Some of our people were polite, thinking it would help the inspectors come to a different decision, some were rude and threw them out of the house, and it made no difference whatsoever: in the end, everyone had to move.

But there was always that ingrained habit, set into the minds of generations of Black people in South Africa, which warned us to be polite, be subservient, so that they won't get angry, because they have the power and we have none.

And even though I grew up in a different era, and I voted in that first democratic election and I got a good education and I didn't experience slavery or servitude in my own life, I suppose we inherit not only our hair and our skin colour but also some of the memories of our ancestors. And so even though I grew up being known as the most outspoken and irritating person in my family, well, maybe we all have lots of different people inside us, not just one character: I am sometimes a dreamer and sometimes a nag and sometimes, shamefully, I am silenced.

I asked my lecturer at university for a meeting. Louise was happy to arrange a time, and though it had to be after work for me, which meant travelling after a long day of teaching all the way across town to her office, it was worth it. As soon as I had explained the thing I had noticed, about how the kids in my class didn't know how to look, she started taking down books off her shelf.

"Of course!" she said. "This is one of the most important things in learning. You have to know how to really see what is around you, how to focus and how to deliberately search for information, in order to collect data and then use it. All the important figures in education theory talk about this, but not all of them talk about how it needs to be actively taught to young children. You can't just assume that a child who can see knows how to focus his attention and look. It is something that has to be taught."

And she told me about people like Feuerstein, who had developed these ideas and proved that they work, and she gave me articles written by him and about his work to take home and read. She told me how children with learning difficulties, as well as children who grow up with extreme deprivation, tend to see the world around them in a sweeping, blurred way, and miss out on the details, so they don't notice the important things and they don't learn well.

She was really interested in my art project and asked if she could one day come and see what I was doing. And she suggested that I write it all up as part of my final thesis, because we would have to write a paper showing how we had applied the theories and ideas of Cognitive Education to our actual daily work. She didn't want us to be filled up with theories and not to make it part of our actual teaching practice, because that, she said, is the very opposite of Cognitive Education. Unless it is made relevant, and meaningful, to the teacher as well as to the learner, it counts for very little. And her job, as well as my own, was to show students that what they were learning was meaningful and important.

CHAPTER TEN

Isaac had been in my class for a few months by now, and I knew he was too advanced for the class, but we decided that he shouldn't be in the older class as they were learning letters and sounds and maths, and with his being in hospital every few months, we were worried he would always be missing out on information and would come back from hospital and feel that he had to catch up on all he had missed. We mainly wanted him to feel comfortable, to be able to enjoy his preschool days, because we knew that soon enough he would have to be at 'big' school and do more formal learning and maybe permanently have to cope with writing with his left hand, and also perhaps have to learn to deal with kids who were not so kind to him.

But he would sit there in my class and I knew he could answer all the questions I asked. Sometimes he would look at me and give a little smile, as if to show me that he knew that I knew this was all too easy for him, and he would usually let the younger children have a go at answering. How can a five-year-old be so mature and so generous?

And boy, was he clever! He was speaking three languages now. When he first came to my class he could speak his own language, Chinyanja, and he could speak some English, which I suppose he learned from his parents or back home in Malawi. But having spent a few months in Sandveld, he was already speaking some Afrikaans. It was really amazing to see how this little five-year-old would speak to his mother in Chinyanja and then turn to me and speak to me in English. All the information, about when he was going to hospital next, and how long he would be away, he would tell me in English.

But I worried that he was wasting his time in my class. He could have been learning so much more.

If I could have had it my way, I would have set aside a bit of time, maybe even ten minutes a day, to sit with Isaac and really teach him the kind of things he could be learning at his age. Letters and sounds and numbers, the things he needed so that he would be ready for school no matter how much time he had to spend in hospital. But I couldn't leave the class even for a moment, not with thirty-six kids all running around in different directions.

A month later he had to go back to hospital for another operation, this time on his scalp, to try to repair some of the scars, and he would be missing at least three weeks of school. I asked his mother to come and pick up some picture books and toys so she could take them to the hospital, in case he got bored there.

There is a volunteer, Rhoda, a very kind and generous woman who comes to visit us now and then, and helps out wherever we need, and she offered to take Isaac and his mom in her car to the hospital as well as to visit him every few days and to read him stories.

If I had to write down the names of all the amazing people I meet every day, it would be a long list. The volunteers, like Rhoda, the people who bring us porridge, Patricia the librarian who looks after kids every afternoon after school as if she were their granny.

Frances who takes in every stray or lost child. Lots of them, most of them in fact, are women. You can read into that whatever you like.

* * *

I don't want to complain, I am lucky to have a job, and I am lucky that for twelve years I have had a job that I love. Lots of our people don't have jobs at all.

But this work at Sunbeams is unrelenting. At that time I was the only adult in the class, and with thirty-six kids, there was always one who fell down, one who wet his pants, and someone fighting with someone else. So usually I had to make sure to go to the toilet myself, excuse me, before school started, and at lunchtime when Bertha would bring the food I would ask her to wait with the kids for a second while I ran to the toilet again. That way I could get through the day without leaving the kids alone for a single second.

But even so, there was always something waiting to go wrong. I remember one day, a girl lost her balance on the slide and fell off, and hit her chin really hard. There was lots of blood and she was first crying and then dazed so I was very worried and needed to get her to the doctor quickly. And then, a second later, a child came running to tell me Isaac's bandages were wet and coming off and he was crying in pain in the toilet. I sent a child to get Bertha and Frances, quick quick quick!

And I could see out of the corner of my eye that Devlyn was standing just behind me, peering out, as if he knew something bad was happening and he was scared to look.

We teachers didn't really talk about this problem, we just accepted that we could not be in two places at once, rolled our eyes to each other in sympathy and tried to help each other when problems arose. But on my first visit to Silverleaf School to observe their work I noticed something which I just couldn't get over. In each class there were always two adults, and sometimes even three or four! And the classes didn't have more than eighteen kids each. So the ratio was that there were at all times, at the very least, two teachers for eighteen kids – one adult for every nine children. And in our school, we had one adult for thirty-six children!

It couldn't be right. And it wasn't just about safety either. I could see that every child at Silverleaf School got time with an adult, talking one-on-one, several times during the day. I stood nearby to listen to what the adults were saying, and it was just the kind of thing I was doing with Devlyn: having a real conversation, talking about things they had seen or done, showing them new ways to do things, teaching new words through the games they played.

Talking with Louise at a tutorial about how children learn language through having conversations with adults, one-on-one, really brought home to me what our kids in Sunbeams were *not* getting: the chance for ongoing, everyday conversation, one-to-one with an adult who was there just for them, who would listen, respond, ask questions, answer questions, and encourage more and more talking. However much I might try to do this for them, it is simply not possible to provide enough conversation when there is one adult and thirty-six kids. No wonder they couldn't describe a picture.

I had been feeling quite good about how I was managing to do this with Devlyn, but here at this school *every single one* of these kids was getting time for special attention and conversation with an adult every single day!

What to do. I agonised over this thing. I talked to Frances, and she was sympathetic (she used to be a teacher herself) but she said, "What can you do? The Trust pays our salaries, they have to raise the money themselves from charitable donations, do you think they will have money for more salaries?"

And when I brought up the topic once too often with the other teachers, they got irritated and said, "Enough already, Dolores! Leave it alone already!"

They sounded just like Grandma Rachael when she used to get sick of me nagging her about something. So maybe she was right, all those years ago. But that's me. Dolores the nag. So I thought, well, if that is what I am, a nag, I am going to be the most successful nag ever, and I am going to nag until we get what I think is right.

So I wrote down my idea, and I am not ashamed to admit that I got Louise at university to help me to write it because I didn't want it to sound like a complaint; I wanted it to be persuasive. She suggested that if I arranged the information in a certain order, according to the principles of Cognitive Education, it would be more persuasive.

The order was like this: first the facts, the 'input'. Next would be 'elaboration': my feelings and opinions about these facts. Finally I would add the 'output', my suggestions for making things better. In this way, a person reading it would have the basic information first, and then I would give them a chance to process the information and to form an opinion, and only at the end would I put in the request to do something, to take an action, which would then make sense because I had led them up to it carefully.

So what I wrote to the Trustees was this:

The facts:
   Our children are at risk of being hurt if there is only one teacher in each class.
   The ratio of thirty-six children to one adult is not safe. One person cannot look in all directions at once, nor can one person pick up more than one child who has hurt himself.
   In other preschools there is at least one adult for every twenty children, and in some private schools there is one adult for every nine children.
   It is not only about safety but also about learning. At other schools, children get spoken to by their teachers as individuals or in small groups, and there is research that shows that young children learn language and learn to think by having one-to-one conversations with adults who show them how to talk and listen, and how to think.
   Our children seldom have a conversation with me because I am too busy teaching the whole group, and I am never free to talk to individual children.

My opinion:
   So I think that our children are not learning as well as children who are in those private schools.

My suggestion:
   What I suggest is that we need a teaching assistant in each class.
   This person doesn't have to be a trained teacher. It can be anyone who is kind, and reliable and patient, and who likes children. Someone who can talk

to the children, have conversations with them, help me to keep them safe, and earn a little bit of money at the same time.

***

The funders from the UK had come on a visit to South Africa to see how their projects in Sandveld were doing, so it was easy for Frances to arrange for me to come to one of their meetings with the Trust, and they set aside some time for me to speak in the meeting.

Even though it was what I had wanted, I was terribly nervous. I didn't know them and they didn't know me, and I am not used to speaking to people from overseas. In fact, I spend most of my waking hours talking to children, not adults. The only adults I speak to are people I have known for years, my friends, and people I work with and my husband. And, of course, recently, Louise and my classmates at university.

So speaking at a formal meeting was something I had never done before. I was scared that maybe they would think my English is a bit funny, with all the Afrikaans words we use. And they don't really know how things are here in Sandveld, even though they visit every year. It is not the same as being here every day. But then I said to myself, Dolores, now is your chance! You wanted to make a noise, you wanted to do something different, don't give up now!

So I put on my best dress, the light blue one I bought for Johannes' fortieth birthday party which sets off my skin colour nicely, and my special earrings, and Frances told me I looked gorgeous, and off we went, Frances and I, in Martinus' car, to the meeting.

Frances had met all the people before, she often had meetings with the funders when they came from England, but it was all new and scary to me. Lorraine, who is on the Trust, was there, so at least I knew two people, but everyone else was a stranger and I didn't know where to sit and when to speak.

But it was all very organised. First the funders spoke. They talked a bit about the new primary school they were starting to build, they showed us the plans and it looked really beautiful. I could see what a wonderful kind of school it would be – not just a big shiny building which had got nothing to do with the buildings in Sandveld, but a collection of huts, built low, painted in bright shiny colours, looking like they had sprung out of the African soil or out of the imagination of a child.

I got so excited thinking of the kids in my class going to this school that I almost forgot why I was there, and suddenly it was my turn to talk and my throat got dry and I had to have a sip of Lorraine's water.

But I did it. I said what I wanted to say. I told them how there is no chance of teaching these kids when there is one adult to thirty-six kids, and that at the school they themselves sent me to, Silverleaf, in order to learn how to teach better, it was one adult for every nine kids. This thing, the adult-child ratio, is supposed to be one of the biggest problems in education in South Africa, and if we want to change how kids are learning, we could start right here.

I told them it was about safety but also about having conversations with the children.

I also told them that just in case they thought it would never work, that people who are not trained teachers can't do anything useful in a school, we could try it out for three months. We could have a pilot programme, and if it didn't work I would give up on the whole thing and accept that I was wrong.

It would cost the trust very little money because they could find people who had no work anyway, and who would be happy to have a small job and earn a bit of pocket money.

I made sure they knew that I was not asking for someone to do my job for me. I know how to do my job, thank you very much. I was asking for another pair of hands and another mind.

I was asking for Devlyn's mother.

* * *

Then I handed out the letter I had printed, so that even if they didn't get it from my explanation, they would be able to read my carefully reasoned letter.

There was a lot of discussion about whether Annetjie was the right person. After all, she could not read or write and perhaps she had never had a job in her life. But I had this feeling that she was the one. Having heard her, after her kidnapping, not saying a word about herself and asking nothing more than to know if her kids were okay, I knew nothing that happened to her could shake her out of her devotion to children. That's the kind of person we need to help us here at Sunbeams; we need people who can show our children that we love them, all the time, no matter what happens each day.

I have to say the funders looked a bit uncomfortable, because when I compared our school to Silverleaf I said, "I have to tell you that most of our kids will never be as good at school as those Silverleaf kids because we don't teach them in the right way, and even if we know the right way we can't do it because there are just too many children and too few teachers!"

But the main thing was that the funders understood what I was saying, and they agreed. Just like that! I thought that I would have to nag and persuade and argue and fight for it, but there it was: they agreed to a pilot programme for six months, not three months, for my class and the five-year-olds' class.

I could just see Grandma Rachael shaking her finger at me up in Heaven. "*Jy! Dolores, my kind*, my child, you go too far! These people pay your salary, you can't just talk to people from England like that!"

But I could also imagine her turning away and smiling to herself, as she sometimes did when she was a little bit proud of me anyway.

CHAPTER ELEVEN

Carrying on with our drawing project, once we had talked a lot about colours I started to talk about shapes.

A circle. It is round. We walked around the school looking for other round things, and we found the wheels of a toy car, the wheels on a tricycle, Bertha's pots and pans and lids (she wasn't thrilled with my bringing thirty-six kids to her tiny kitchen to handle her shiny clean pots), plates, the base of the tins in which we kept our crayons. We traced the shapes with our fingers.

I asked the children to trace circles in the air. We blew bubbles using diluted dishwashing soap (Bertha again) and we looked at their shape. More circles.

Then I asked them to draw circles. Believe me, some of them couldn't do it at first. They just didn't know how to start, and how to plan it on the page, and I could see some of them were not really looking at their page but were looking at my circle which I had drawn on the board as an example.

I knew that four-year-olds should be able to draw a circle because I asked the kids at Silverleaf to draw circles and they could. Part of the difficulty for such young children is not knowing how to hold the pencil correctly and part of it is learning how to coordinate their hand with their eyes, and those were things I could help with. But there was more to it. My children were not familiar with what shapes looked like, and what they were called, and what the difference was between one shape and another, so how could they possibly draw any specific shape?

So I stuck sheets of newspaper on the walls and we drew huge circles, and I showed them how their whole arm could go around in a circle, like a helicopter, which they recognised because a few months ago someone arranged for a helicopter to land in our field, the field where the new school will be, and all the kids went to see. Then I put a drawing of a circle on a piece of paper next to each child, so they could look at it without having to look up at the board on the wall and away from their own paper. For those who needed it I guided their hands, and after a while they could all draw a circle.

I held their drawings up, next to an orange. "Look! It's the same shape! An orange is a fruit, it is round. Its shape is a circle, and you drew a circle shape! Now you can draw a round orange."

I drew other shapes: a square, a star, and we talked about how those were different shapes, they were not the same shape as an orange which was a circle shape.

I put one orange on each of the five tables, made sure there were enough orange crayons for each of the six children at each table, and they looked at it and began to draw.

So with that we had our first figurative drawings. Maybe it is not creative, but these children were starting to learn how to really look.

After that I added other fruit to our still life (again having raided Bertha's stores) starting with a banana, to show them how different the shapes can be from each other. I held up a banana and we talked about it. I tried to find as many words as I could to describe it, because one of my targets was to help these kids to see that everything, whatever they see or feel or experience, can be talked about in words. We talked about curved, and bent, and long, like a moon, like a cupped hand, like the roof of a car. I gave them strips of cardboard, cut out of cereal boxes, and they bent them and curved them and looked at the shapes. Then I asked them to lie on the carpet, to lie straight, like a ruler, and then to lie curved, like a banana. And afterwards they drew bananas and we talked about the colours, and they used yellow and coloured them in.

***

I wanted to be sure that every single one of my kids knew the names of several colours and also of some basic shapes. I got this idea from my diploma course, because Louise had mentioned that knowing how to use descriptive words, like words for colours, shapes and size, is as important as learning the names of objects. So this is the game we played, for a whole week, day after day:

I cut out of cardboard (old cereal boxes which I asked the parents to send in) three different shapes: circles, squares and triangles. I had big ones and small ones, and I painted them different colours. Then I showed them to the children, and we named each colour, each shape, each size, carefully, over and over.

The game we played was to put them all inside a bag, and each child had a turn to put their hand in and take one out, and he had to say what colour it was, and what shape, and what size. For those who didn't know much English, I let them say just a word, just the colour or the shape. But for those who knew more English I wanted them to say the full phrase: 'big red triangle', or 'small blue circle'. I made it a bit more fun because I had a turn too and made deliberate mistakes, and the children had to catch me out, and each time they caught me out in a mistake I had to do a penalty, like run around the class, and they thought it was hilarious that they could tell their teacher what to do and make her look ridiculous and out of breath, so I had their full attention for ages while they learned to look and to name.

* * *

I was still obsessed with getting the kids to look at things, and to say what they could see. So now when I collected the drawings they had done each day, I put the pictures up on the wall at a child's eye height, and before the end of the school day we would walk from one picture to the next, looking and describing. I made sure to say whose picture this was, and to describe the shapes and colours the child had used, and then I asked the child to say what he had shown in his picture.

Slowly the conversation started emerging. And what a difference. They were looking, they were recognising their own pictures, and they were telling me what their picture showed; they were even talking to each other about the pictures, describing them, saying which they liked and why.

It probably doesn't sound like much to you. You are probably used to kids doing this kind of stuff. But for our kids, believe me, it was something new.

And don't think it was all about art. I also wanted to get them to use their looking and observing outside the classroom. I noticed that when they went outside, all they seemed to do was a lot of running and chasing. Not that there is anything wrong with that, but it seemed so repetitive to me. Of course they needed lots of outside active play to let off steam and to develop their muscles and fitness, but when I thought of the kinds of things I used to play outside when I was a kid, it seemed sad that my kids didn't seem to know any games.

So the next day I put two big laundry baskets on the sand outside, and asked the kids to line up behind them in two rows. I gave each child a 'bean bag', which I had made the previous day from some of our ever-present beach sand tied into the toe of an old sock.

As I have probably already told you, we may be short of toys and crayons but one thing we are never short of here in Sandveld is beach sand.

"Throw the beanbag into the basket," I told the children. And they stood, looked at me, and threw.

Of course, if you are looking at your teacher you can't throw a beanbag in a basket.

I explained how to do it. I said, "Look! Look at your hand, look at the bean bag, look at the basket!" and gradually they got it, they learned how to aim. I got them taking turns, standing in line, and they got better and better at it.

I'll say this again – you are probably thinking, what's the big deal, surely all children can throw a ball in a basket? But mine had never done this before, and aiming at a target is not something you are born knowing how to do. You have to have the equipment, and you have to have someone to show you how to do it, and you have to practise.

Then I added some beanbags made from different coloured fabrics, and I gave them longer instructions:

"Throw an orange bag first, and then a blue bag!"

"Throw two bags the same colour!"

"Throw two different bags!"

"Throw an orange bag, clap your hands, then throw a blue one!"

Devlyn could only do one instruction at a time, and he and some of the younger kids had to have the laundry basket brought a bit closer in order to be able to aim properly, but most of the others could listen carefully and remember longer and longer instructions, and they simply loved it and didn't want to stop, even though Bertha was there with the day's fruit snack: more oranges.

One of the teachers, who taught the class with the three-year-olds, liked my idea and borrowed two big squashy balls and tried it out with her class. I walked by just as one of the kids was trying to work out how to pick up a ball. He had never held a ball in his life. He didn't know how to bring his two hands together towards the ball, how to cup them so that they would hold the ball and it wouldn't fall out of his hands. He tried, incredibly, to use the backs of his hands – maybe he didn't like the feel of the ball? And slowly, patiently, his teacher shaped his hands and helped him to do it, and after a little while he picked up a ball and threw it, and beamed, and everyone clapped.

* * *

We had one month at the end of summer when it was particularly windy, even more than usual, and we started to hear about a new problem at Overcome Heights. The recent winds had blown the sand onto the roofs of some shacks, which were now sagging more than ever, and the weight of the sand was threatening to push over the flimsy walls. There was a photo in the local newspaper of a shack with the wall leaning over so far into the house that it is a miracle the roof hadn't fallen in. One woman had been stuck in her house because the sand had piled up outside her door overnight and in the morning she couldn't open the door and had to call to passers-by to help her get out.

One of the residents told the newspaper reporter that the city council used to clear the sand before it reached so high, but that had stopped a while ago and now the sand was just piling up and up.

Not only that – the sand was getting into people's food, and people trying to cook had to keep everything covered because even in a few minutes sand would get into the food and it was impossible to eat.

Talk about chaos. Those people had so little, not even a proper house, and just when they thought they at least had walls and a roof, a bare minimum of what you need in life to feel safe and to keep the elements at bay, the sand itself turned against them.

CHAPTER TWELVE

After the Trust agreed to pay for the two assistants, I asked Frances to talk to Devlyn's mum and explain it all to her, and ask if she wanted to take it on. She had to explain to Annetjie that if she agreed, it would be for four hours every single day, no days off, Monday to Friday. We wanted her to know that she would be paid at the end of each week, and that I would explain to her every day what she needed to do, and I would be there with her and we would help each other.

At first she seemed not to understand that we were actually offering her a job. It turned out (I wasn't surprised to hear it) that she had never had a job. She had lived from hand to mouth, had been with a man for a while who had a job, so she had enough food from the time when Devlyn was about eighteen months, then some time later she lived with the gang member and they had a lot of money for a little while, enough food for the kids, and clothes too, and then she was on her own in that shack in Overcome Heights. Now, suddenly, she not only had a room to live in with a proper roof and a dry floor, but she was being offered a job! With money, sure money, every week the same, no surprises. She sat there looking stunned and then, calm as anything, said, "OK, I come." And she got up, there and then, tied the baby on her back with a blanket, and waited for us to lead her to her job.

"Hang on a minute," said Frances, "not so quick. First you have to speak to the Trust, they want to interview you, and you have to sign a contract. Then you can start working."

I could see Annetjie's face just closing down and at first I couldn't understand why she was upset. She sat down with a bump and the baby started to cry.

"No, no," cried Frances, "let me explain again, it is for sure, it is a real job, they just want to say hello to you, to meet you!"

Then in a flash I got it. She probably didn't know how to write her name, and signing a document must have been the most daunting thing she was being asked to do. So I quickly said, "You don't have to actually sign, I will read it to you and when you listen, and understand, and if you are happy, I will show you where to put an X, and if you can't do it, Devlyn will show you how!"

Devlyn was sitting nearby, and I didn't think he had been listening, but he looked up and gave his beautiful smile. I took his hand, and together we drew a big X in the sand.

Well, I am sure it is not entirely legal to have a child of four sign documents for his mother, but this is not an entirely normal country either, and if it takes the kids to teach the parents, well at least somebody is doing it. And what's more, both Frances and I now had clear evidence that Devlyn could understand what was going on around him, because he started to draw X's in the sand, all by himself.

It was smiles all round after that.

* * *

On her first day of work, Devlyn's mother came into the classroom led (almost by the hand) by Frances. She was clearly terrified, so I made sure to give her some very small but specific jobs: clean the tabletops with this *lappie*, sit next to me and listen to the children singing, make sure they wash their hands after they go to the toilet. Slowly, as the day went on, she seemed to relax, and I started to see where Devlyn got his beautiful smile.

The other assistant we got was Charlene. She was a neighbour of Patricia, our librarian, and would sometimes come in to help us if any of the teachers was off sick, or once when Bertha was away visiting her daughter who had just had a baby up North. Charlene was sweet, kind, outgoing, and friendly to everyone. She had had a hard life, but who hasn't in this town? Her husband was into drugs and was on the run for a long time and then got caught and is in jail now. Her daughter was at school in the next suburb, up the road. Irene was then seven years old, in her second year at school. She sometimes used to come to Sunbeams after school if Charlene had been helping us, and would wait for her mother and they would go home together. In a way you could say that Charlene was one of the lucky ones, she had a house which was given to her by the Trust when they built proper brick houses and allocated them to 1600 families in Sandveld.

That is a separate story, the story of the 1600 houses, and I can tell you that later, if we have time.

***

Once Charlene started working as teaching assistant at Sunbeams, her daughter Irene started coming to us every day after school and would wait for Charlene to finish work so they could go home together. Even though their house was just four doors away, Charlene didn't want Irene to be alone in the house. Not with all the bad things that happen to young girls here in South Africa. So Frances made her a space in the corridor, with a little table where she could sit and do her homework after school each day.

Irene was always neatly dressed in her school uniform, a white shirt which, amazingly, was always clean even after a whole day at school, and her hair was carefully arranged in corn rows.

Sometimes she would come to my classroom, when the kids were having their nap, and sit with me doing her homework while I was writing my notes. We would sometimes look at the reading books she had been given by the school. She was still struggling to read fluently, and while she could read the easier words, she could not read the longer words and seemed not to be able to make sense of what she had read.

She would often come home with a book she had already read a few weeks ago, and I started to realise that the school didn't have enough books to provide her with the variety she needed. I was sure she could do better, learn to read more fluently, and that she would enjoy it more if she had a variety of books with different kinds of stories in them.

I asked Charlene how Irene was doing at school. Charlene said, "Mixed. Sometimes good, sometimes not so good." Irene's teacher had told Charlene that Irene was a very good girl, no trouble at all, but when Charlene looked at her written work she was surprised that at age seven, in her second year at school, Irene was still spelling most words incorrectly. She was also reading very slowly, with lots of errors, and Charlene was quite worried.

I was amazed, just chatting to Irene, how mature she was, how she understood why it was important to do her homework every day, and why Charlene had to work so hard instead of spending time helping Irene with her homework or just playing with her. "My ma, she is the best worker! You see, Miss, she just works and works and that is why we got money to have our own room and I got a nice duvet, I am never cold at night! It's because of my ma, she just works and works! When I will be big, when I finish school, I will work just like her." So for such a bright child, who was so much more conscientious than I had ever been, it was surprising that she was not reading well.

I knew it wasn't my business and it definitely wasn't my job, but I arranged with Charlene for Irene to come to my classroom every day when my children were having their nap. We would sit on the paved area just outside the classroom, so I could still keep an eye on my kids, and go over her homework. Usually she had managed to do some of it on her own, and her handwriting was really neat and careful, but I could see she was having some difficulty like confusing 'b' and 'd', and that she really hadn't learned any of the spelling rules that kids her age should already know, for example what happens when you add an 'e' at the end of a word like 'bit'.

I know it is harder for our kids, those who speak Xhosa or Afrikaans, to read and write in English, and I know that they shouldn't have to, that they should first learn in their own home language, but in Irene's school there was a decision to teach in English, and a lot of the parents were happy with that because they felt that if a child knows English really well they have more chance of finding a job when they finish school.

If I had to teach all the children in my class in their home languages, I would have to know about five more languages, and I would have to repeat each thing five or six times each time I explained anything. So at Sunbeams we too stick to English as much as possible. It's just practical.

Anyway, I asked Patricia at the library to ask around and find out who could give me advice about teaching English reading and spelling to a seven-year-old, and two weeks later along came a woman who was trained in teaching reading to children whose first language was not English. She had learned a special method that was being used in the townships around Cape Town, a method developed by a charity called Wordworks, and they were so generous, they allowed her to spend about five hours with me, spread over a few weeks, just showing me how to teach using their method, and giving me all the materials I needed. I got letter cards and flashcards with pictures, and little books with stories and cut-out characters, and I didn't have to pay for a single thing.

So that's how I became Irene's teacher too.

I don't want you to think I am something special, that I am especially kind and generous or anything. It's just that here in Sandveld, women help each other. And Charlene had helped me out so many times, coming into my class if I was called away for anything and once when Johannes was in hospital and I wanted to visit him. Patricia invited Charlene to join the library and choose suitable books for Irene, so that she was not limited to the books from her school. We are all in this together.

And anyway, once you know something, once I had learned how to teach English reading, there is no way to undo what you already know, so I used what I knew to teach Irene.

* * *

You can say what you like about the way I teach my kids, maybe I am too pushy, maybe I don't let them just play enough, maybe all these theories from university have gone to my head. A few people have told me this and I haven't had an easy time keeping my theories going.

But one thing you have to agree, and nobody can disagree, one thing I have done which has made a difference is to get those two teaching assistants, Annetjie and Charlene. Because you can use any teaching method you like and you will struggle to get good results if you have one teacher for thirty-six kids who are not yet five years old, but you may have a chance if you have one teacher for eighteen kids.

And maybe one day we will even have one teacher for nine kids, like at the private schools. And then we can compare like for like and you will see what our kids can do.

END of PART ONE

PART TWO

Comparing and Categorising

CHAPTER THIRTEEN

Well, as I said, the course I was doing at university was an eye-opener for me because it was showing me a kind of teaching which was totally unlike anything I had ever seen. But at the same time it made me a bit uncomfortable, because I didn't like to think that everything I had done in my twelve years of teaching, which had taken so much of my energy and effort, was somehow wrong, and that all those years I had been depriving my kids (already so deprived) of something they had a right to.

I think everyone in the tutorial class was feeling the same way, and occasionally we talked among ourselves about this, but we had signed up to it and as a group we decided to trust the process and to see where it led us.

One of the things that really helped was the way the lecturers put things over, because in teaching us they used the exact principles they were trying to get us to use with our own students. They did everything they could to make the method meaningful for us as individuals. They gave us lots of examples from our own daily lives, instead of just giving us lots of theories which we couldn't relate to. They called this 'bridging', meaning that they were creating a bridge, a link, between the theory they taught us and its application in as many other areas of life as possible.

Louise spent a lot of time talking about Cognitive Functions: all those things that we do with our minds and our thinking that are skilled and efficient and useful. She talked to us about how there are many different kinds of thinking which people use in order to be good at what they do.

It doesn't matter if you are a teacher, or a bus driver, or you are buying new shoes, or you are a student at university – the same kinds of thinking skills are needed if you are going to do those things efficiently. And these are the thinking skills which would help our children learn to read and write and do maths as well as to solve problems and to make wise decisions in life.

She asked us each to tell the group one thing that we do really well, and that we love doing, and then she analysed for each of us what thinking skills, or what 'Cognitive Functions' in her words, we were using to be good at that thing. One of the students told us about the charity she had set up, going from one grocery shop to the next, collecting food that is reaching its sell-by date on that same day and asking the shops to donate the food to her.

She doesn't even have a car, she does this with an old supermarket trolley. Then she wheels the full trolley to the subway crossing under the main road in Claremont, where she knows many homeless people spend their nights, and she unpacks the food and leaves it there. She told us that she doesn't usually meet the people who eat her food as they are usually not there during the day, and anyway she doesn't go right into the subway because she is scared of being a lone female in a deserted place. But sometimes she sees one of 'her' homeless men and without fail he raises his cap to her, bows low like a court jester, and says, "*Hey! Meisie! Baie dankie*! Thank you very much!" and he gives her a huge toothless smile.

The lecturer asked her how she came up with the idea, and she said she bought some cheese from a grocer and it was past its sell-by date, and when she brought it back they were very apologetic, and said of course you can exchange it for another one. And when she asked what usually happens to this food, they said, some manufacturers take it back and sometimes we have to just throw it in the garbage, but we usually eat it if it is just one day past the sell-by date because there is nothing wrong with it.

"Aha!" said the lecturer. "You are using a cognitive skill called 'collecting information'. If you didn't have that knowledge, you wouldn't have known that this food is going to waste. Please carry on."

So then the student told us that when she left the shop that day, a homeless man was sitting on the side of the road, and she regretted not having just offered the cheese to him. He obviously needed it much more than she did!

"Comparison!" said the lecturer. "You compared your needs to his, and realised something. Comparison is one of the most basic thinking skills we have, even small children have it when they say, you gave a bigger piece of chocolate to my brother, it's not fair! Please go on, tell us what you did next."

"Well," she said, "I thought about it for a while and remembered that there are three grocer shops in our suburb, so I went to speak to them and asked if they would be willing to give me some of their out-of-date food, but only if it is still in perfect condition, only one day after the sell-by date, for me to give away. When they agreed I started to think how to carry all this food, because I don't have a car, but I saw an old supermarket trolley which had been thrown into the river and I asked my very strong younger brother, who likes to pretend he is a cowboy, to lasso it and pull it out, which he did. So we cleaned it up and I made a cardboard sign saying 'The Good Food Organisation' and tied it on the side of the trolley, and I started collecting and distributing.

"Aha! Another cognitive skill. We call it labelling, giving something a name. Tell me, why did you make a sign for the trolley?"

"I was scared people would think I stole the trolley, or that I stole the food, and also my parents' neighbours are always running to tell them all the bad things they see me doing (they once caught me smoking in the field behind the school) so I wanted people to see I was doing something serious for a change, something legitimate."

Louise explained that what she called 'labelling' is just the same as when a small child learns his first words: he realises that a word can stand for a thing, and that if he wants to get that thing, or he wants people to look at that thing, he just needs to say that word. So this student needed to call her trolley by some formal words to make people understand she was doing something important and organised, not just walking around town with a trolley full of food.

Well, that I already knew about, because I had now spent a whole two months working with my kids on naming things. Even Devlyn was getting better and using more words now, and my older kids were more and more able to describe what they saw in the picture books I brought them from Patricia's library.

So gradually, probably in the same way that my kids were gradually learning to see the world in a new way, I was starting to understand what Cognitive Education meant in a new and more organised way. I was feeling a bit less bamboozled after each lecture, and I was starting to get the whole idea.

It's not that these ways of thinking were something magical or new. We all use them, in more or less efficient ways. It's just that I had never thought about it in that way before – as something that needs to be explicitly taught to children in school. The point is, that it seems that children who are not learning well don't have these basic skills, and as Louise then proceeded to tell us, children who live in extreme poverty never have the chance to learn these skills, because life for them and their parents is so stressful, there are so many emergencies every moment of the day, that nobody can perform at their best no matter how competent they would be in other circumstances.

Louise wasn't finished with that food charity student yet.

"I am thinking about all those things you did before you started actually distributing the food. You found out who would donate, you worked quite hard getting the trolley fixed up. You obviously are very skilled at this. You used your planning and problem-solving and organisation skills to find the food, to get agreement from the grocers, to find a way to transport it, and to get others to help you when you couldn't do something on your own."

She was trying to show us that thinking before you act, and choosing carefully what to do first and what to do next, is one of the most basic and important skills a person can have. That Cognitive Function is called 'planning'. It doesn't matter what you are doing: setting up a charity, or baking a cake (you have to have a recipe, buy the right ingredients, add each ingredient in its correct order, leave the oven on for a specific time), or catching the right bus at the right time going in the right direction so you get to work on time. You have to plan first, you have to be organised, if you want things to work out well.

That really made me think, because one of the things that I think Grandma Rachael was best at was organising. She organised everything and everybody. She organised the annual Christmas decorations at our church and the New Year parties for every 2nd of January, which is a special festival for us in the Coloured community. She organised her neighbours' shopping trips by making them tell each other when they were going shopping, so that a mother who had young kids at home could get a neighbour to do some of her shopping for her if she couldn't go out, or a neighbour who was staying home that day could look after the kids for a few hours while their mother went out. She organised me, my whole life, so that from the moment I got up until I went to sleep I knew what to do and where to go and how to make myself a meal, even when she was away at work all day long. Of course not everybody welcomed Grandma Rachael's organising their private lives, but in the end we all knew if you wanted to get something done you should ask Grandma Rachael.

I could also see why some of the children came to school without warm clothes, with no spare trousers in case they wet themselves, even though we told the parents over and over how important it was, and how embarrassed their children were when they had to wear clothes from our pile of spare clothing. It wasn't just that the kids didn't have warm clothes, because we made sure that if a child didn't have a warm jacket or jumper, we gave them one from the collection of kids' clothes which was brought to us each month by a local charity. But with some families, even when we gave the child a jumper, two days later he would turn up at school without it, and when we asked what had happened to it, he would say he didn't know where it had gone. It was a matter of not being organised.

I also noticed how some parents were not organised enough to pick up their kids from Sophie at the Shebeen in good time for them to get home and have supper before dark. Sophie used to be exasperated by this, because she had a business to run, and it was in the later afternoon and evening, once the kids should have already been picked up, that crowds of men started to come to the Shebeen and she wanted the kids out by then. When she asked one of the parents, who was repeatedly late, he told her that after work he went with his friends for a little walk, he walked with them to their bus stop, and then he missed his train... there was always a reason why he was late and it wasn't because he had to work late or anything like that, it was because he just couldn't organise his time.

And I saw it in the kids themselves: if we asked them to tidy up the toys before putting the tables out for lunch, they just threw everything in the big box, all mixed up, so that afterwards I had to go through it all and sort out the Lego from the cars.

So I decided. From now on, all the things I did, all through the teaching day, would be about showing the children how to get organised, and how good it is when things are organised. Organising our time, organising the space around us, organising our ideas.

We teachers already had a daily timetable, written out and stuck on the wall of every classroom, so we could all start at the same time, and coordinate the toilet breaks in shifts to prevent all the kids in all the classes going at the same time. We also had to organise our time, because Bertha had to know when our activities ended so that she could start cooking and provide lunch at the right time.

It sounds obvious, and maybe it is, but I had never thought of this: that we teachers used the timetable to organise our day, but we didn't make any conscious effort to show our kids how or why we needed a timetable. We adults took organisation in time and space for granted, but what we needed to do was to show the children not only how to use a timetable, but also why it was so helpful and important.

As Louise kept saying, "It's your intention that counts! You have to know clearly what you intend to teach, and it's not enough that *you* know, your students have to know too! And if you don't make your intentions clear to your students, you won't achieve what you wanted to achieve. And if your intention is to help them be more organised, you have to show them why it is important, and show them how to do it, not just do it for them."

* * *

I started with how we organised our day. One morning when the kids came into class, I just sat there and didn't do anything. I greeted them but I didn't get up, didn't say we are going to sit in a circle and sing, I didn't do any of my usual stuff. So of course the kids were a bit surprised, and confused. A few of them came up to me and said, "Miss, what are we doing now? What are we going to do?" I said, "I don't know, what do we usually do first thing in the morning?"

Well, of course they knew, because one thing I am good at is having a really structured and consistent classroom routine, so they said, "First we sit in a circle and say hello, and we say how are you, and you write down who is here and who is sick."

"Aha!" I said (I learned that from Louise), "So we have a *plan*! And do you know where that plan is? Here it is on the wall!"

And I took the timetable down off the wall and showed them the numbers which would tell us what time to do things and the words which were there to tell us what to do. I showed them that we start at the top of the page, and that's the first thing we do each day, and we move down, so that by the end of the day we have done all those things.

I had made a new timetable with a column down the right-hand side, and I covered it in transparent wipe-clean plastic, so that each time we finished an activity we could tick it off and check on the timetable what was next. And I left a space at the top of the timetable to write in what day it was. And all during the day, and every day after that, when we had finished any activity, or when it was time to eat or to go home, I asked two of the children to come with me to check the timetable, tick off what we had done, and decide what we needed to do next.

And that's how I started teaching my kids about how to organise their time.

* * *

What Louise had said about making our intentions clear not only to ourselves but also to our kids stayed in my mind. It was not just learning about routine and how time can be organised, but showing the kids *why* it was so important. I started to pay much more attention to describing what was in my mind as we went through the school day. Instead of just having a plan for the day, or a new idea about something useful to teach, I would talk aloud about what I was thinking – why it would be fun, what the purpose of the new activity was, how it could help us.

It was a kind of window into my mind that I wanted to provide for the kids. I had to model this kind of thinking for them, and show them how my mind was working, so that they could see that organising your day and your time was helpful, and useful, and pleasurable, and that the opposite was confusion and chaos. So I would say, "Hmm, we have been drawing for a long time. Let's see, what is the time? I better look at my watch. Oh! It is nearly ten o'clock, what do we usually do at ten?"

I would wait for the children to answer, to remember our routine, and then show them on the timetable that they had remembered correctly, that after drawing came snack time. I used words like first, and next, and before, and after.

And don't think we stuck to it rigidly, because that's not realistic: we were flexible too, and we had some lovely discussions with the whole group about what to do if the timetable said it was time to play outside but it was raining, and we talked about how we sometimes had to change our timetable and couldn't play outside because we would get wet, so instead, we could have a snack a bit early and maybe play outside later. So words like 'earlier' and 'later', and words like 'prefer' and 'instead of', and 'choose' and 'decide', became familiar to children who usually could only talk about what was right there in front of them. They were starting to think about the situations we found ourselves in, to make choices, and to tell me why they had made those decisions. That is quite something for a four-year-old to do.

Every morning we used our weather chart to look at the weather, to talk about what it was like, and what we could expect from the day's wind and rain, and to plan our day as a group instead of me, the teacher, doing all the planning and missing those opportunities to teach my children to think for themselves. I sprinkled all my talk to them with phrases like "hmm, we have got a problem" and "let's think first" and "let's make a plan, we need to think of a good idea, what can we do now that it is raining?"

Slowly, the children started to understand that each activity we did, each decision made, had some thought behind it, and a good reason for doing it, and that you can stop and think about the best choice you can make. And one day, when I was watching three of my boys making sandcastles at break time, and struggling to produce the right mix of sand and water to make the thing stand up and not collapse, one of them said, "Wait a minute, let's think, maybe it is too much water? We need to do it another way."

CHAPTER FOURTEEN

One of the things that had been worrying me for a while was how the kids behaved when a visitor came to the school, especially if it was someone they had never seen before. They would watch the person for a while and the minute they saw that the visitor was friendly they would mob her (it was usually a woman). They would grab her hands, and try to hold on to her sleeve or shirt, and call her to watch them jump or run or slide. The visit would sometimes descend into chaos. I remember with humiliation one visit, when the woman sat on the floor with a child who was doing a puzzle on the carpet, and all the children just mobbed her, jumped on her, pushed her over, until her spectacles flew off and I had to help her to get up. She was shocked, and so was I. How could my lovely kids, who were usually so gentle and fun-loving, behave like this? It wasn't that they were trying to harm her in any way – on the contrary, they just seemed so desperate to get her attention that they lost control.

I talked to them about this over and over. We talked about how to behave with visitors, and I got the other teachers to come into the classroom so we could role-play how the kids would behave. But it worried me, because I couldn't put my finger on why such a thing should happen with my usually well-behaved kids.

I asked Louise at university, and to her credit, she admitted she had no idea, she hadn't seen anything like this before, and she asked for some time to think about it.

A week later, before the lecture started, she asked my permission to talk about this in the class. I was at first a bit worried about it because it made me look like an incompetent teacher, and it made my class look like wild kids. But in the end I thought, this is such an important thing, maybe it is happening with other teachers and they are too shy to talk about it. So I agreed.

What Louise said was that perhaps children living in extreme poverty, whose parents are away most of the day or are themselves unable to cope with life in an organised way, had never learned about how social systems are organised. Middle-class children are usually taught by their parents and at school about rules, the rules of playing games like checkers and snap and the rules of playground behaviour, like taking turns and, perhaps even more important, waiting for your turn even if it takes a long time. And without rules and organisation, life is chaos. Children need calm and order and some predictability in their lives if we expect them to learn how to control their emotions and to think before they act.

It made me think of Devlyn, because even though we didn't know anything about how his early years had been, I suspected that they had not been good. So how could I expect him to sit calmly, to listen, and to learn? Maybe he was looking around, ready for action at a moment's notice, because he didn't know what would happen next.

Louise wasn't finished. Social rules, she said, are one of the best examples of organisation, because without rules society cannot function. There are rules for where you are allowed to put up a house, and for which side of the road you are allowed to drive on, and for how you treat other people. And the worst thing that apartheid did, besides the murder and torture of our people, was the breaking up of the structures we had in our society, of our families and our tribes and our groups of neighbours, so that we were prevented from living by the old rules and values and beliefs of our communities, and now we are trapped in poverty and chaos and the only place young people can find some kind of rules and organisation is by joining a gang.

Well, that made me think, I can tell you. We were uncomfortable, the whole group of us listening to Louise, because she is a White woman and we thought, how could she possibly understand all this, but it seemed she did, and she was trying to find a way to help us help our kids to get some kind of rules and organisation back in their lives.

When all our friends and family had to move away from District Six, all the traditions and structures and the family support systems and the good neighbourliness were gone in a moment, and people were moved to places where they didn't know anyone, where there was nothing familiar, and it felt like their whole life had been torn up into little pieces and the pieces were scattered all over the Cape Flats and everything that had been before was gone.

So when I thought about it, the idea that rules are a way to organise our lives seemed right to me. I decided to try to include that in my teaching programme.

I would start with a game, something really fun that the kids could play, to show them that the game has rules and it is fun if you follow the rules. I knew it would only be possible to have a rule-based game outside, in the playground, because our classroom was too small for all the kids to play any game all at the same time, and it didn't seem like it would be much fun if only half of them could play at a time and the others had to be kept busy doing something else.

So I started with hopscotch.

The kids had never seen hopscotch before, but I used to play hopscotch with my friends when I was a young child. It was one of our favourite games and we played it at school in the playground as well as after school and on weekends. So I drew a hopscotch grid on the paving outside our classroom, using chalk so I could rub it out afterwards, and demonstrated the hopping and the counting. We had been working on the numbers 1-10 in class so many of them were familiar with these when I wrote them in the squares, although some of them, including Devlyn, had not really grasped numbers yet. They were, of course, keen to start hopping, and it got a bit chaotic and after a short time in which they had hopped and jumped all over the squares, the chalk had been rubbed out and nothing was left.

My first real opportunity to show them why organisation mattered was right in front of me.

"What happened to our squares?" I asked.

"Miss, it got rubbed, Miss, it's gone, we can't play any more!" they shouted. Some of them were visibly upset.

"What can we do so that won't happen next time?" I asked them.

Of course, they said, "Draw it again", and I had to explain to them that if we all just jump all over the place it will get rubbed out over and over, and the chalk will get used up and we won't have that game ever again.

"BUT!" I said, pausing dramatically, one finger in the air, "I have got a new idea. What if we do something different? What if we go carefully, and slowly, and take turns, one at a time not everyone together at the same time, and we are careful NOT to jump or walk on the lines? We will jump OVER the lines! Then it can last for a long time!"

And I demonstrated how I could jump over the lines, without touching them, and the lines were not rubbed out. I hoped they would see that thinking about our actions before we do them, and moving carefully, and following the rules, was a way to bring order to our game, to make sure the lines would not be rubbed out. "First think!" I said to them. "Is it a good idea? First think!"

There was a longish silence. The silence itself told me that this was sinking in: they were thinking about how doing things one way caused a problem, but doing them in a different way could be better.

That was a big lesson for my kids to learn.

The next day I walked my kids around the school, debating the best place to draw the hopscotch grid. We couldn't have it just outside the classroom, where all the kids gathered at the start and end of each day, because how could anyone play when all the children were standing there? And we needed a paved space, because how could we draw on the sand? We talked about how to choose a suitable flat paved space, out of the way of the tricycles and the kids running out to the playground.

I included my children in every step of the planning, because I wanted them to see how planning and thinking before you do something can help you to do it right.

I was impressed how seriously the kids took these discussions. They were thoughtful and helpful and we finally agreed on a spot which was paved but which didn't have lots of traffic during playtime.

I drew the squares, put in the numbers and found a small stone. Then we had to decide who would go first, and in an attempt at showing them a different way to organise things, I decided that the kids should line up by height, with the smallest in the front.

Well, that took some time too, because it involved everyone measuring themselves against everyone else, and there were a few arguments among kids who were of similar height and I had to arbitrate. I also noticed how Devlyn seemed not to grasp the idea and he just agreed to stand wherever he was told to. Isaac, of course, stood aside quietly for a while, waiting for the squabbles to be over and for the line to form itself, and then quietly took his place in his correct position.

The kids were itching to start, and were fidgeting and practising their hops, so it was not easy for them to wait while I told them the rules, the counting, the position of their feet, where to turn around, and I also had to remind them not to throw the stones anywhere other than onto the squares.

But it was worth the effort, because slowly I saw them taking it in, managing to control their impulsivity and their impatience, and believe me it was not easy, not for me and not for them.

But we got there in the end, and everyone had a turn. All the other teachers came out to watch, and I felt like the conductor of a band, making sure the rules were followed and everyone got their turn.

We were not surprised, though we were disappointed, to find that by the next day, the wind and the sand had rubbed out our chalk lines. Of course it was Isaac who suggested that maybe, if we drew the lines in paint, it would last for a long time. I tell you, that boy didn't need me to teach him to use planning and to solve problems.

We asked Martinus to source some paint and to go over my chalk lines one Friday, so that by the end of the weekend the paint would be dry and the lines would be permanent. Hopscotch became one of the most popular games at Sunbeams, and we even had to paint two more grids on the paving because so many kids wanted to play.

Every day, we had to sweep the sand off the hopscotch field, because it got completely covered over with sand after a few hours. You could say it was a real nuisance, the wind never stops and the sand is just everywhere, but I saw that the kids would stand around while I swept, waiting for the lines to reappear, and when they did, it was as if they were seeing them for the first time; their eyes grew bigger, they shouted out each number as it reappeared, and they cheered when the whole thing was clear. So even the sand was teaching them something: to wait, to control their impulsivity.

So, you may ask, what's the big deal? Anyone can play a children's game. And how can I say that such a simple game, so common among children all over the world, can be part of an educational programme for kids living in poverty? Well, I'll tell you what my kids have learned from hopscotch.

They have learned to wait their turn, and to follow the rules of a game. They have learned words for direction and for position (forwards, backwards, jump over the line not on the line). And they have learned that you have to think about the things you do, not just do whatever you feel like at the time, and to think about the consequences of your actions. These are big lessons for a small child to learn.

* * *

Louise had talked a lot in her lectures about the 'intention' a teacher has when trying to teach anything. She wanted us to be sure, every time we taught something, that we were able to explain to ourselves, and to anyone around us, and to the children too, just *why* it was important to learn this thing.

So even though I had shown all my colleagues, even Frances the principal and Bertha the cook and Martinus, how to play hopscotch, I wanted to be sure that everyone really understood that it was not just a game, it was part of this new method of education I was studying.

And I thought that maybe this idea about bringing order into our kids' lives could be more than just something I did in my own class with my own kids. It was a kind of project that the whole school might want to join in with, and maybe they would all make it part of their teaching and part of their children's lives too.

So I wrote out the rules for hopscotch on a big piece of cardboard and put it up in the corridor, next to Frances' office door, to make sure that anyone visiting would know that we are not just playing; we are doing Cognitive Education here at Sunbeams.

How to Play Hopscotch:

*The first player throws the stone onto the first square.
After you throw the stone, look where it has landed. If
the stone does not land in the correct square then you
lose your turn.*

*The player then hops over that square to the next
square. Keep hopping to the end of the field, turn
around and come back.*

Pick up your stone on the way back.

*On double squares you must land with both feet at the
same time, one foot in each square.*

*If you have completed this with no mistakes, you can
have another go and throw your stone onto the second
square and so on.*

*You must wait in line and only go when it is your turn.
Never push another child.
Be careful when you throw a stone, it can hurt someone.
You must only throw the stones onto the ground.
Look carefully at the lines! You must not step on a line.
Look carefully at the numbers! Go in the correct order.*

* * *

And still, it wasn't enough, said Louise.

What now? What more could I do? Everyone would
get sick of hopscotch before long if I kept on adding
more rules. But Louise said that it wasn't just about
writing out the rules, although that was important
because rules help us organise our lives and our society.

But the rules still don't explain why hopscotch is important. I still had to explain my intentions and my reasoning: *why* was it so important for the kids to play hopscotch? I had to be able to justify the time it was taking, and also the fact that I was getting my kids to spend so much time on what was just a game, instead of using that time for teaching letters and numbers.

If nobody knew what this game was trying to teach, what my intention was, then the whole activity was a waste of time, and was nothing more than a fun game.

I thought about it. At first my intentions had been simply to teach the children to wait their turn and to play according to the rules.

But Louise said that wasn't enough. She wanted me to be able to explain to her and to the tutorial group, using the language of Cognitive Education, exactly *which* thinking skills the children could develop if they played hopscotch. So I made another list, because, as she told us, if we had in mind, in our intention, the specific thinking skills we wanted the children to learn, and if we made it clear to them what these were, then they would have a chance to really learn them. Louise wanted me to use the technical term for thinking skills, 'Cognitive Functions', which I wasn't entirely comfortable with as I thought nobody would know what it meant, but anyway I did it because she was going to mark my paper and I wanted to get good marks. I can't really explain why that mattered to me but it did.

And, as she kept reminding us, having the intention in our mind wasn't enough either! If we kept our intentions only in our own minds, and didn't make them clear to the children, then that is where they would stay: in our own minds only.

So I sat down that evening and made a list of all the different types of thinking you can learn from hopscotch. I know it is just a lot of jargon if you aren't familiar with it, but by that time I was starting to know what it meant and to feel comfortable with it. Anyway, I wanted to show this to you so you get an idea that even though the actual activities I was doing with my children may seem to be really simple and nothing special, there was a lot of theory behind it, and actually I feel quite proud of myself for being able to understand and remember all of this. I think it does show that I can adapt to new ideas and learn new methods even if I have been in the same job all these years.

What hopscotch can help children to learn:

Knowing what you must look at in order to play correctly (Cognitive Function: Attending to relevant information)

Counting: knowing how to read the numbers and knowing how to count to eight (Cognitive Functions: Labelling; Cardinal and ordinal numbering)

Following rules about the sequence of things, what happens first, next and last: what you do first is throw the stone, next you hop over it, then you turn around, then you come back again (Cognitive Function: Sequencing)

Following rules about direction of movement across the hopscotch field (Cognitive Function: Orientation of movement and position in space)

Knowing what happens if you make a mistake (Cognitive Function: Hypothetical thinking: using 'if')

Waiting your turn (Cognitive Functions: Following rules; Reducing impulsivity; Respecting other people's space; Planning; Thinking before acting)

Don't step on the lines, and throw your stone carefully (Cognitive Functions: Systematic search for a defined and specific target; Accurate perception; Accurate output)

Checking and reflecting on your actions. Have you achieved your goal? What can you do next time to improve your aim? (Cognitive Function: Evaluation).

CHAPTER FIFTEEN

In the morning, when the kids come in, they each have a hook on the wall with their name written above it, and they hang their coat and their school bag on that hook. This is nothing special, most preschools have this system. But Devlyn could never do this: he would come in and stand still until I went over to him, took off his jacket, and hung his coat and bag for him on the hook. Every day, day after day, I would say, look Devlyn, this is your hook, here is your name, you need to put your coat here, you need to put your bag here. And day after day he would just stand there, waiting.

I still didn't have any idea why he was so passive, and why it was so hard for him to do what all the other children of that age could do: take off your coat and hang it up in the correct place. But with my new-found enthusiasm for this idea about organisation, I thought I would try to teach a different organisation skill to the whole class, and maybe Devlyn would hear my explanations and respond to my new way of teaching, and maybe he would start to join in more.

Our work with the timetable had been about organising time, but the coat hooks were about organising the space around us, and that is something a bit different. The more I thought about it, the more fired up I became by the idea of organising our space. I walked around our school and looked for things which could be better organised.

I thought, how about the buckets and spades? They were usually to be found strewn all over the playground (our playground being one gigantic sandpit, you remember, no grass, no trees, just sand) and sometimes the smaller children couldn't find anything to play with, so no wonder all they did was run and chase each other. Each day we teachers had to walk around searching in the sand for something for our kids to play with. We were all supposed to collect the toys at the end of each day, but with that sand there was always something missing, and after a few weeks we would notice that there were no spades to be found anywhere.

So I thought, maybe we should have four boxes of playground equipment, one for each class? Or even one big box, and every day, after break, all the kids could pick up all the buckets and spades and balls and put them in the box, so that the next day each teacher could take some equipment and give it to her kids at break time.

And what are numbers for, if not to organise things by counting them? So once the spades had been found, together with the kids in my class I would count them, and count the buckets, and in front of the kids I would write the number on the big storage box, like this:

Buckets: 9   Spades: 17

With numbers on the box we would know how many spades and how many buckets there should be, and if one was missing we would know, and we could keep looking for it.

Even better: How about if I organised a giant treasure hunt, where all the kids had to go around the playground and dig in the sand and search for spades, and those who found a spade would get a huge cheer and get to stand on the podium (a little box which Martinus cobbled together out of scrap wood) and receive formal congratulations from Frances. And we would explain to all the kids that the reason we were so happy and proud was not just because they found the spades, but because now we could tidy the buckets and the spades into the special new box and we would know where they were when we needed them. And that way the kids would know why we were doing all of this, what our intention was, and – hopefully – understand how that kind of organising could make things much more fun when they wanted to play.

We did the same with our toys in the classroom. I put the Lego in one box and labelled it in big letters 'Lego', and the cars in another and labelled it accordingly. And I made sure that every child knew, and could tell me, *why* I needed to do this.

Because now I truly believe, and I hope I can make our children believe too, that if you are not aware of why we need to organise our world, and our possessions, and our time, and the space around us, life will continue to be chaotic. And you can teach as much maths and reading as you like, but if you don't teach them about organising and planning and thinking, their lives will not change much. It's not just for our kids either: I think everyone needs to have some order and a little bit of predictability in their lives. And here in Sandveld, with all the wind and the leaking roofs and the gangs and the violence and not always knowing if you will have dinner that night, our kids need predictability more than anyone.

***

Bertha, our wonderful cook, was a willing participant in my attempts to teach the children how to organise their world. She was only too happy to have two or three kids with her in the morning when she took delivery of the day's vegetables and meat and porridge, and to show them how she worked out how many carrots to use, and how to make sure the kitchen was clean because otherwise the children might get sick, and what time to start cooking so that the food would be ready on time. It wasn't as if she had a proper kitchen either – all she had was a corner at the end of the corridor which had been walled off to keep kids from going near the stove, but she made space in her heart and in her daily work to give my kids some sense of forward planning and problem solving. "What can we do? No carrots today! We need vegetables, vegetables make us strong and healthy. Let's think, what other kind of vegetable should we have today?"

So Bertha too started to think aloud, and to create a window into her mind and show the kids how she thought about and planned and organised her work every day.

***

Meanwhile I was still visiting Silverleaf School once a month. I was curious to see how they taught their kids to notice the world around them, and name what they saw, and if their children understood how their teachers organised their day.

And secretly, I wanted to see whether they were more organised than we were at Sunbeams. Sure, they had better equipment, more space, everything was new and shiny, but that didn't mean they were teaching their kids in a better way.

One thing I saw, and I just loved the idea, was a special timetable not just for the whole class but for a child in the school who had learning difficulties. This child could not keep up with the activities everyone else was doing because he had Down Syndrome, and I could see how his timetable was helping him not only to learn about time but to be able to stop an activity he was doing and do something different, and that was not easy for him because he sometimes liked to do the same thing over and over. So he got to do a whole range of activities in his day, instead of doing just one thing all day.

His timetable was different from mine: it was pictures only. His teaching assistant (another adult in the room!) had lots of pictures showing the activities he could be doing and she would stick four or five of them, the pictures for the tasks of the day, on a horizontal strip of Velcro; she would show him the pictures before he started any activity, and at the end of every single activity they would look at it again, to show him what he had just done, take down the picture of the activity which he had just finished and put it in a little box, and then look at the timetable to see what they would be doing next. So he learned about first and next, and start and finish, and he learned that his day could be planned and orderly.

I could already anticipate what some people would say: that we teachers were constantly interrupting what the children wanted to do and imposing on them our own wishes, and we were stopping them from expressing themselves and from playing, which is what children in preschool are supposed to be doing.

We had had a visit from an exchange group of teachers from abroad and they had been shocked at the physical conditions, the poverty. It is easy for any visitor to see that we have too few toys and too much sand. But when they came to observe my lesson they were more impressed when they saw us singing traditional songs with the kids than when they saw me discussing the timetable, and trying to stick to it during the day.

In fact I came in for a bit of criticism, which surprised me and I wasn't prepared for it so I couldn't think of a good response. But talking about it with Louise a few days later I was even more surprised to hear from her that this kind of teaching that she was promoting, Cognitive Education, was not always admired or even accepted in many other places. She had often been told that her kind of teaching was enforcing too many rules, it was intervening in a child's natural development, and even imposing Western values on other cultures, which we had no right to do.

She gave me copies of articles which had been written about this, both for and against this kind of teaching. We had hours of discussion in our university tutorials about it, and I don't think I can even begin to tell you about all the heated debates going on in the world of education and academics. I started to see how many political and philosophical differences there are in this field, and how different countries and even different schools within those countries have their own beliefs and philosophy of education, which means that they teach in very different ways.

But here in Sandveld, here in Cape Town, I know one thing: our kids live in a raw and dangerous world of poverty, drugs, gangs and violence. And unless they learn to plan, and make sensible choices for themselves, and think about how to solve their own problems, nothing will change for them and they will continue, for generation after generation, to be illiterate, getting involved in gangs and drugs and killing each other.

That is not why we struggled to release ourselves from apartheid. Freedom of that kind was not what we fought for.

So yes, we intervene in our kids' thinking, and we don't let them just do free play all day long, because there is something more urgent that they need.

CHAPTER SIXTEEN

What those visiting teachers said about being too rigid and rule-bound stuck in my mind. After I simmered down and stopped feeling hurt by their comments, it did make me think. I do agree that you need a balance, and if your routine is too rigid that is also not good, because nothing happens in the way you think it will: your plans may fall apart at any minute, and if you are not flexible enough to come up with a new plan, then you just won't know what to do. And young children do indeed need time to play, to have fun and explore, and to learn in their own way, in their own time.

But play is not enough. Children need more than to be just left to their own devices.

I started introducing choice in my class. In our craft sessions, the children were usually offered a range of materials. We would put out lots of craft materials on the tables where they were sitting and they could choose anything they wanted, cutting and gluing, or drawing or painting. But now I changed that. I made sure to show them first what was available, and to give them some time to think about it, so they would not be making impulsive choices. They had to think about it, and ask for what they wanted. That is when I realised that what we had to offer was a bit limited – always the same things, some recycled paper, some crayons and old magazines to cut up.

So I put out a call, via Patricia as usual, for scrap materials – paper, card, ribbons, glitter and glue – and her lovely volunteers took big cardboard boxes, covered them in bright orange paper and labelled them 'Stationery and Craft for the children of Sunbeams Preschool, Sandveld', and they put a box in front of every shop and supermarket in the wealthy areas around Sandveld: Fish Hoek, Simonstown, Kalk Bay. They put little ads in the local newspapers and spoke to some church groups in the area and material started flooding in.

We got so much stuff that I had to give some away to other preschools in Sandveld, and it was taking me and Annetjie so much time to organise and sort that we drafted in Irene and Isaac and set them the task of being responsible for the stationery cupboards.

That sounds like child labour, but actually the two of them had a marvellous time discussing how to group the materials. By colour? Or separating paper from card? And should they make up a bag for each class or keep it all in one stationery cupboard for teachers to take as they needed? And all these discussions were evidence for me that these two at least were using their cognitive skills; they were organising, and grouping, and using hypothesis and evaluation. I pushed them further: "What if we give more materials to one class than to another, will it be fair? Is this the best way to do it, or can we do it better another way?"

So when these two in a few years' time need to use their reasoning in maths or science, they will certainly be prepared for that kind of high-level thinking.

Trying to give the children the opportunity to make choices was not that easy when it came to toys, as we didn't have that many. Take Lego, for example: we had one smallish box of Lego pieces, too few for even two children, playing together, to really construct anything. There just was not enough. To make matters worse, we had been given donations of building bricks which were of various different makes and none of them could fit onto each other.

I set the older children in my class a task: to decide how to share out the Lego. I asked them to come up with a way to make it fair, so that everyone would have a chance to play properly. I started them off with a hypothesis: what if I give one piece of Lego to each person in the class? How many children do we have? Thirty-six? Well then, all I need is thirty-six pieces and everyone will get one piece of Lego and they will all be happy!

At first there was silence, because they thought I was being serious, but slowly they started to understand the issue, and you can imagine the scorn with which my idea was met. We had a bit of a laugh, but I kept on at them until they could explain to me exactly *why* my idea was silly, and then I left them to decide how to arrange things in a better way.

They came up with some really sensible ideas, like giving all the kids at one of the tables one week to play with Lego in any way they wanted, after which the Lego would move to the next table. And they suggested talking to the children about sharing, so that no single child could take all the pieces at his table.

We tried it out, but after a while we could see that it was not working, because there were simply not enough pieces for even six children to play at the same time. We talked about it as a whole class, thinking about what we had tried to achieve and why it didn't work, and they came up with a new rule: every day, only two children at the Lego table could play with the Lego, and the other four had to wait for another day.

This new thing, allowing the children to decide how to solve problems like the Lego shortage, became really important in our class, and I started to see how authoritative I had been (in the nicest possible way) in dictating the rules for behaviour in the class. Not that I was going to condone anything which was unfair or unkind, but I realised I had never explained *why* I imposed the rules I did. I needed to be much more transparent, to show them how my mind worked when I was choosing a rule for behaviour, so that they would learn to think for themselves and make good decisions when faced with conflicts when no teacher or adult was around.

I desperately wanted to give all of them, but Devlyn especially, the experience of making choices for themselves. Devlyn was doing so much better, in so many ways: he was speaking a little, and he was fitting into the daily routine, and even listening and paying attention a little more, but he was still essentially a passive child who would do whatever he was told, and never made choices of his own.

I was impressed at my kids' attempts to solve the Lego problem, which frankly didn't really have any good solution, but I was happy because in essence the ideas were their own and they had used problem-solving skills which I would never have expected of them.

And all this was carefully written down by me to present to Louise and my tutorial group a few days later, as evidence of the potential of these amazing kids, and what they could do when given some cognitive tools to use. Thinking, planning, solving problems. And all because we were short of Lego.

I wished those visiting teachers from abroad could have seen my class then, because I am sure they could not have been anything but impressed.

* * *

I got a good idea from a DVD we were shown at university. It showed a teacher who had found a way to create a quiet place in each classroom, for those children who wanted to sit and look at a book, or for those who needed somewhere to get away from the rush and crowd and noise of a busy classroom.

It was quite a simple idea: she simply took long pieces of fabric and hung them from the ceiling to the floor, to separate off a little corner of the room. Then inside that space she put a soft mat on the floor, and some cushions, and a little box with a few books.

This teacher hung up some little fairy lights, and used beautiful fabrics, and a thick, soft, furry carpet, all in neutral colours to keep the children calm and relaxed, and that meant having some money to spend. We didn't have money, but the idea was good, and Martinus was only too happy to find some hooks and put them in the ceiling, so that one corner of the classroom was sectioned off, and Patricia had had a donation of someone's old curtains so we used the lining of those, which was a neutral beige colour, to divide off the space. We used the actual curtain fabric to cover an old duvet and put it on the floor as a soft mat. Once Annetjie and I had created this secret quiet space, we put a few books on the duvet and stepped back and said nothing, watching to see what the kids would do.

And sure enough, they crept in, one by one, and later two by two, quiet as mice, and just sat there whispering to each other. Somehow the separateness of the space, and the softness of it and the neutral colours, gave them a message of calm and quiet. Over the weeks we started to see that those children who most needed quiet would find themselves a space there. Isaac especially loved it because he felt safe there without too many boisterous children around him who might jostle his bandages, and Devlyn would sit there, quiet as a mouse, looking at books. Calm, relaxed, not like a *mossie* any more, darting from place to place, but quiet as a bird in a nest. Something about that space gave him a feeling which was different from whatever it was that made him so restless everywhere else.

I was really happy with that corner. It seemed to help me to bring order into my classroom, by dividing and organising our space: there are places to make a noise and other places where we can be quiet.

* * *

I said I would tell you the story about the 1600 houses here in Sandveld, so I had better tell you now.

Don't think that just because the gangsters who kidnapped Annetjie are from somewhere else, not from Sandveld, and just because we have so many good people here, like Frances who takes in lost children, and Sophie at the Shebeen who makes sure children are safe after school, that we don't have our own problems right here in Sandveld.

We had a very bad time a few years ago. And it was all about trying to make a space for people to live in, in fact, ironically, it was about trying to organise our space, just like I was trying to do in my classroom.

What happened was this. In the beginning, Sandveld was just a place on the dunes where *trek* fishermen had their shacks and could keep their nets and boats. What *trek* fishermen do is to row out to sea with a huge net, which is weighted down, and drop it there, and later they come and stand on the beach and pull the net in to see what they have caught. It is a huge job because the net becomes terribly heavy, and often they have to bring in other people to help, and crowds gather on the beach to see what has been caught and often to buy fresh fish, straight from the ocean.

Over the years more people, not just fishermen, came to live in the area and built their own shacks on those dunes. Originally most of the people living there were Coloured, but after a while other people came to live in Sandveld: people who had moved from the Eastern Cape to find jobs in town, as well as many people who were refugees from other African countries. During the apartheid times they were always being harassed by the police and their shacks were pulled down as fast as they could build them, but after some years the police stopped bothering to bulldoze the shacks and the town grew bigger and bigger.

There were no drains for sewerage, and there were only about twenty water taps for the thousands of people living there.

Something had to be done. There were two groups who wanted to represent Sandveld to the City Council. One of them was our Sandveld Development Trust and the other was a group led by a local man and his supporters, and they had a kind of war between them.

There was lots of anger and there were threats and violence each time one of the groups seemed to be taking charge or having a meeting.

And in the end, when building permission was granted and money had been collected by donors from overseas to build brick houses and to install a proper water supply and sewage disposal, and everyone was celebrating the first few real houses being built, two of the young men working for our Trust were shot dead. So that war of words had become a real war, and some people thought that the matter of allocating houses to poor people was a matter of life and death, or rather, just death.

* * *

In the end 1600 new houses were built, and Charlene lived in one of these and Annetjie's new home was going to be in a room in another of these houses. So the outcome is good, even if it was terrible along the way. And really, when you think about it, it was all about organising our space, the space where people live.

One of the funders who donated money for those houses was asked if he thought it was worth all the trouble and pain and the death of those two fine young men, who were leaders of the community and had worked tirelessly to get proper housing for the people of Sandveld.

And what this donor said was that he was not the one you should ask, because he doesn't live there, but when he asked the people who do live in Sandveld, usually what people would say to him was that before the housing and the plumbing, every winter old people and children died of cold and exposure, and children's health was threatened by lack of clean water and waste disposal. And the new housing has saved so many lives, maybe those two had to sacrifice their lives for this.

So, I wanted to say to Louise, things are not so simple. Sometimes, those very thinking skills which seem so wonderful, trying to organise your space and your surroundings, can lead to big trouble. And just when someone is trying to bring order to our lives, it can end badly. It is all very well to say that our lives need more order, that our town could be more organised, but now you can see how some people worked very hard, for a long time, and they ended up getting shot.

CHAPTER SEVENTEEN

The next Sunday, Annetjie was due to move her things out of the shack at Overcome to the room near the school which the Trust had organised for her and her kids to live in. Martinus had offered to help her with his car and I went with him because I wanted to be there, just to be encouraging and perhaps to hold the baby or to talk to Devlyn while she packed up.

I was shocked when I saw how few belongings she had. They were what you would need for a life on the move: one pot, some wood for a fire, two blankets, mattresses to sleep on, a few nappies and clothes for Devlyn and the baby, a few bits of her own. No furniture, no spare shoes, no ornaments, nothing personal.

We drove off, Devlyn watching the road passing underneath Martinus' car with fascination, and arrived at Annetjie's new home. As we started unloading the car, Patricia wandered up the road to welcome them, and quickly assessed, in her efficient way, what Annetjie needed. Later that day the support team, Patricia's volunteers from the rich suburb on the other side of the highway, arrived. They brought food, a small cupboard to keep the food in, warm blankets, a bucket to wash nappies, and toys and books for Devlyn.

Annetjie was overwhelmed – she had never seen so much stuff and didn't know what to do with it. But Devlyn, bless him, had clearly learned something with all my talk about getting organised, because he arranged in a corner of the room a little space for his things, his new toys and books and clothes, all neatly stacked in little piles. And then he helped his mother to pack the food into the cupboard before going outside to look at his new surroundings.

***

Looking at Annetjie and Devlyn together, the resemblance was striking. They both had that gorgeous smile with teeth slightly too big for their mouths, but they were also both unusually small and thin. So maybe Devlyn's size was not something caused by malnutrition, but just a family resemblance. Or maybe both Annetjie's and Devlyn's small size were caused by malnutrition.

Louise had directed me to some research about children's development if their mothers don't have enough protein and vitamins during the pregnancy, and I read a lot about it. I knew that malnutrition could have a very serious effect on Devlyn's learning: it could lead to difficulties with attention and concentration, as well as with memory and problem-solving and even behaviour.

But each research paper also said, very clearly, that the problems caused by malnutrition can't be separated from the problems caused by stress and violence and homelessness and illness and all the other things that Black people in South Africa have suffered from, so we couldn't be sure if it was the malnutrition that led to his problems or something else. Probably it was all of those things combined.

I also read a lot about children with foetal alcohol syndrome, whose bodies and brains were damaged by their mothers drinking too much alcohol while they were pregnant, but by now I understood Annetjie well enough to know that was the last thing she would do, that whatever had happened to her, whatever was done to her, she would never have done anything to harm her babies.

In one way, all that talk with Louise and my fellow students at university about organisation and planning and logical thinking worried me. Of course, it is easy to see how it must affect a child's life, and adults' too for that matter, if their lives are chaotic and random and disorganised. I could see how some of the problems people face in their daily lives could maybe become slightly less overwhelming through being more organised.

But most people living in Sandveld and Overcome Heights have little choice in the matter. Nobody chooses to have a leaking roof, or to worry about their child joining a gang, or getting sick.

And though I could see how Devlyn was struggling to learn anything because his concentration didn't last long enough to really listen to or look at anything I was trying to show him, the idea of talking to him about being organised seemed ludicrous. He probably wouldn't even understand what I was saying. What he really needed was a roof that didn't leak, and warm blankets and good food, and to feel safe. And now that he had those things, who knew what he could do next?

***

At work, Annetjie would watch me all day. Her eyes would follow me around, and she tried to learn how to be a teacher. I wonder how it felt for her, how big a change it must have been for her to move from her previous life, and how things had now changed for her and her kids: she had a home, a salary, she could plan healthy meals, and they would be warm and relatively safe at night. She sat with Frances now and then asking for advice on how to budget her weekly salary to make sure she first bought the necessities and then the rest.

And a change in Devlyn really was becoming apparent: he seemed to spend less time looking anxiously around, and he was able to settle down to playing with one toy at a time for quite a while, instead of moving like a butterfly from one thing to another. And he was growing a bit too; his trousers were too short.

***

It is true that sometimes things in our lives are chaotic and random and terrifying, especially here in Sandveld, but sometimes it is not like that. Sometimes things just happen in a good way.

It turned out that someone had donated a huge sum of money to our school, so that we could get rid of the worst and most leaky containers and have two more brick classrooms, with proper insulation.

I haven't told you yet about what the old classrooms, in those shipping containers, are like to work in. The walls are metal and there is no insulation, so in winter they are icy – literally, there is ice on the walls – and in summer you feel like you are being baked in an oven. We had an expert come in to advise us, and he suggested we cover the inside with wood panels with foam insulation between the metal and the wood, and that outside we paint the metal with reflective paint to keep the summer heat out, but nothing had been done. It was all too expensive and there just wasn't the money for that kind of luxury.

Where the containers had been joined together there was usually a leak. In the worst classroom of all, where my colleague Brenda was teaching, the walls were sometimes so damp that even though she stuck the kids' paintings on the wall using a special tape, by the end of the day the pictures would have slid down the wall and would all be lying in a heap on the floor. Besides which it was always cold in that room and the kids had to wear a sweater and sometimes even two. In winter Brenda used to teach with gloves on all day, and in summer they had to leave the door open to get some air, and our resident dog always managed to sneak into the classroom and flop down right in the middle of the floor and shed some of his fleas there. So the news about the new classrooms was really exciting.

It was also great news for my kids, even though we already had a brick classroom. Because from the beginning of that building project I got my kids to watch and learn from the builders, and it became part of my daily lessons. How did the builders decide where to put the new classroom? They looked, they measured, they discussed, they planned. This was organisation and planning happening right in front of our noses.

So instead of keeping the kids away from the builders, which maybe I should have done because building sites are not such safe places to be, I got them watching and even asking questions.

I suppose it was irritating for the builders, they just wanted to get on with their work and they didn't need thirty-six little kids buzzing around, but I set very firm rules for where the kids would stand, and made sure they would not go over the line which I laid out in old bricks on the sand, so they would be standing in a safe space. I also made sure to bring mugs of tea to the builders during the day, and even some cake one day when one of the volunteers brought us some goodies, to sweeten them up so they would agree to let the children watch and even answer some questions.

So my kids learned. They learned that to start a building you first have to measure, and for measuring you need to know your counting and your numbers. You need to dig a deep hole for a foundation, because if you don't, the walls will fall over. We practised doing that in the sand, at break, using scrap cardboard for walls, and sure enough, if the kids put their card deep in the sand, it would take a really strong wind to blow it over, and if they just stood their cardboard pieces up with little support, they would blow over at the first gust.

I got the kids to watch when the bricks were being delivered, and we noticed how one man stopped the traffic in the road before they started offloading, so that no cars would by mistake crash into the truck delivering the bricks. He organised that road. And we watched how the builders stood in a line, passing bricks along the line and up the scaffolding, so that nobody had to carry a huge heavy crate of bricks all by himself, and by being organised, by standing in line and each person taking their turn, all the bricks were where they needed to be by the end of the day and the truck could drive away.

Just like when we stand in line to play hopscotch, or wait our turn to go on the slide. Rules are not there just because teachers say so, but because it makes things work properly and helps us have a nice time.

So all through those months of the building project, my kids watched and learned while the builders measured and planned and built.

***

Winter came, and with it a driving rain which never seemed to stop. The wind blew so hard that the rain seemed to fall horizontally instead of from the sky to the ground, and where should it find its main target but the join between the two containers, which had always given problems.

Brenda, the teacher, called me in to look. She had the children sit on the drier side of the room because the floor directly under the join was flooded and she had buckets there to catch the drops of water. The electric lights gave out, of course, and the kids were learning in this damp, dark, cold space. It was heartbreaking to see them trying to draw pictures when all the colours, the reds and the yellows and the blues, looked a dull grey. Especially when we had those two brand new brick classrooms, now almost ready, to compare to. But we couldn't move into the new rooms yet, they still had to be painted and to have ceilings installed.

We had to find a solution in the meantime until the new rooms were ready. Frances called Lorraine, who called the other members of the Trust, and they also called James, the businessman who had for years been advising the Trust on financial matters, and they came up with a plan to temporarily use another shipping container, which was considerably newer than ours and which had been placed in a neighbouring field as a youth centre.

But meanwhile the children were upset, and disrupted, and disruptive, and it was a hard time for their teacher, who did not have a teaching assistant in her class and had to cope with the move all on her own. We 'lent' her Charlene for a few hours, to help her move all her equipment and her kids to the new container, and Charlene alternated with Annetjie, and (sneakily) I sent a message via Frances to thank the Trustees for providing us with these teaching assistants because they were helping the other classes too, and I mentioned how wonderful it would be if each class had an assistant.

Well, you have to try, don't you?

CHAPTER EIGHTEEN

Finally the building was completed and we had two new classrooms. And when the Trust said they wanted to have a party in the new classrooms, I hijacked their plans, I'm afraid, and made it a special project for Irene and Isaac. Together we organised the party: Irene carefully wrote out the invitations and we discussed what time the guests would arrive and decided that each one of my kids, even Devlyn, would personally greet each guest and accompany them to the new classrooms, and all the children from the two older classes would then sing them a welcome song. So now the idea of bringing order and planning to Sunbeams school would be something everybody would know about.

All of this tied in beautifully with the next topic Louise had moved on to, which was 'Comparison'. She wanted us to see how all that work about looking carefully, and listening, and learning the words for what we saw and heard, is just the start – it is the way we collect information. But what do you do once you have the information? The next step is to organise that information in your mind so you can think about it. You process it, you elaborate on it.

She reminded us about the student in our tutorial class who had set up the food distribution charity, and how she had compared the food which had reached its sell-by date with fresh food and decided that there was a short space of time in which the quality of the food was actually the same, so it was safe to distribute food which had just passed its sell-by date. That was when I first heard that comparison was something to do with learning and thinking and planning.

We learned, in our Cognitive Education course, that one of the most basic ways to think about information is to compare one thing with another. We were given endless examples of how choosing carefully, by comparing all the options, can help us make wise decisions. The examples our lecturer gave us were simple ones, which would apply to anyone's own daily life: which laundry soap gives better value for money (the bigger pack or the cheaper one?); which shoes should we buy (high heels or low? fashionable or comfortable?); how do we choose a career (teaching or office work?) or a friend (trustworthy and loyal or just a person to have fun with?). All of these choices need us to compare one thing with another before we can decide.

Most kids learn to compare at a very young age. They compare big and small ("I want that big piece of chocolate cake, not the small one!") and they compare old and new, clean and dirty, happy and sad, yummy and yukky. But children with learning difficulties, and children who live in deprivation and violence, often don't automatically learn to compare, and they need to be specially taught. I suppose it's because for people who are very poor, there usually aren't many options to choose from, or to compare with each other. You make do with what you can get hold of, and you don't have the luxury of choosing something else which might be better.

So now my task was to introduce this new thing, comparison, into my teaching, in a way which would help my kids to start using comparison in their own lives. Comparing things would make it possible for the children to decide what was important and relevant and what was not. It would make it possible for them to notice when things changed in their surroundings and to be able to know what those changes meant, and to talk about them, to compare the new with the old.

We walked around the old classrooms and then went to compare them to the new ones. That meant comparing wet and dry, old and new, as well as the benefits of having more space, more windows, of having brick walls instead of metal walls, of having bright lights so we could see what we were drawing rather than old weak lights where we could hardly see each other.

One week there were problems with the vegetable deliveries to the school, and this became the basis for a lovely few days of lessons in my classroom. I asked Bertha to come and explain why vegetables are important, and then she asked Martinus to go out in his car to the local 'posh' delicatessens, and he managed to get the delis to donate an example of some unusual vegetables which my kids, with their food supply limited to what was available in the local traders' roadside stalls, had never seen: spaghetti squash and yams and parsnip. So, we could talk about and compare the different vegetables: their shapes, their colours, their size and taste and texture. Parsnips are just like carrots in shape, long and pointy, but a different colour and a different taste; spaghetti squash is not real spaghetti, real spaghetti is made of flour and water, but it looks the same! And it tastes different! So we were able to add that very important Cognitive Function, comparison, to our daily menu.

***

We were all curious to hear how Annetjie felt once she had settled into her new room, and how different it felt when she compared it to her previous place. We decided to give her a housewarming party, so on the first Sunday afternoon after her move we each baked something, and we brought paper cups and paper plates and popped in and visited her. She was overwhelmed and initially could not say a word. But gradually she relaxed and smiled, and Devlyn came out from behind her skirt, and we had a lovely party and we each talked about how it felt for us, having Annetjie as part of our team, and how she was helping us and helping the kids.

I told everyone how teaching had been such hard work before Annetjie came to help and now I had someone to share the work and it was such a pleasure. That was something I could compare.

She told us about how Martinus had fetched her that day from Overcome Heights, from that house with its broken roof and no floor, and how different that house was from this house. And how well Devlyn was sleeping these days, now that they had proper walls and a door, and they all felt safer.

Just sitting there with Annetjie, we noticed how many things we could compare. Before and after. Broken and fixed. Vulnerable and safe.

Comparison is a big deal in Cognitive Education and I can see why.

***

After Annetjie had worked with me for a few months, and had relaxed into the job and started to feel more comfortable with me, she told me more about her life before she came to work with us, and how she worried that Devlyn had those problems because she didn't have enough to eat when she was pregnant. And that may be the reason, but when I thought of that life they had led I could see there were plenty of other reasons too. Living from hand to mouth, scared of her partner, never knowing if the roof would leak or if someone would break in, never having enough clothes and food, a life where nothing could be planned and you never knew what awful thing would happen next. How could it not have affected Devlyn? No wonder his attention was so fleeting, no wonder he kept moving. You can't catch a moving target.

And now Devlyn was starting to pay attention for longer periods, and they were all, Devlyn and Annetjie and the baby, so much better off. Not just in terms of housing and safety and food and a job, although those of course came first. But also in terms of being able to plan their lives, to live more predictable lives, to notice what was around them and to compare and to make choices.

Of course, I am not naïve. I know that in Sandveld, with all its problems of poverty and crime and drugs and poor health, chaos is always just round the corner, but we were just so happy for that little family.

You may think, how could I take a woman like Annetjie, with her history, someone who probably never went to school herself and who couldn't even read or write, who could barely look after her own children at one time, and entrust her with the job of teaching assistant? But I had a good feeling about her, I can't tell you why. And when I watched her sending off the kids at the end of each day, making sure they were wearing their warm jumpers and had their bags securely on their backs, and I saw how she gave her beautiful smile to each child, and gave each one an encouraging word, I knew I had been right.

***

One of our volunteers brought along a neighbour of hers, Debbie, who wanted to see what was going on in the township across the highway from her house on the other side. First they visited Patricia at the library and she told them the whole story of the Sandveld Development Trust and the 1600 houses, and how she had started the library from nothing.

Then Patricia brought them to visit us at Sunbeams. We wanted to take Debbie to see all the classrooms, especially the new building, but she took one look at the littlest kids, the two-year-olds, who were at that moment having their nap, and then she just stood there and didn't want to see anything else.

Then Debbie said quietly, "Thank you, I am going home now."

And with that, she left.

We didn't know what to think – perhaps we should have been more friendly? But we are always so busy, there really isn't as much time for being as sociable to visitors as we would like.

Well, it turned out that she had immediately noticed that even though the kids had blankets, there were not enough blankets for each child so they had to share, and some of the blankets were a bit small so some kids were not really well covered, and it gets really cold in those shipping containers.

So Debbie went home and phoned all her friends and persuaded them to crochet blankets from scrap wool which Debbie had a cupboard full of, and a week later she arrived with sixteen exquisitely colourful stripy warm blankets, one for each of the two-year-olds at Sunbeams. And she stayed until their nap time and took a photo of them all sleeping soundly under their rainbow blankets.

CHAPTER NINETEEN

Patricia, the librarian, popped in to visit us one day while we were supervising the kids in the playground. As you can tell from the number of times I talk about her, she had become a good friend of our school, always just around the corner and happy to chat and help us solve problems. While we were chatting that day with Frances, she mentioned that she had noticed, now that winter was coming with its rain and cold, how many children came into the library without shoes.

Now that is nothing special here in South Africa. In summer many people, not just children, and not just poor children, are happy to walk barefoot. I see people going to the supermarket barefoot, and not just in Sandveld either, but in the rich suburbs too. But in winter this place can be bitterly cold, especially when it's blowing, and the sand which is usually so soft and flyaway turns to yellow mud. Walking barefoot in the damp and cold is horrible.

We talked idly about the cold, and the mud, and about the local shop, Pop Stores, which was having a sale of school shoes because the school year was already well under way and everyone who was going to buy school shoes had already bought theirs.

You can see how ideas arise, just from a few women chatting. So who knows whose idea it was, and what does it matter? We decided we three would try to raise some money and buy shoes for those children whose shoes were broken or too small.

Before we sent off any requests for funding we needed a catchy name for the programme, because there are endless appeals for help and support for poor children in South Africa, and how can anyone be persuaded to get excited about yet another appeal? Frances, Patricia and I went back and forth, throwing out ideas and names, but we couldn't think of a name which had the right ring to it.

Until Irene came home from school, and listened to us talking, and said, "Miss, can I say? I got an idea."

Irene's idea was so simple and so perfect. "You are talking about these kids with no shoes, well they are barefoot, aren't they? So call it Two Bare Feet."

And so we did. Patricia was off, in her usual energetic way, like a beam of light, making her way down the road to the library to phone 'her' volunteers. Frances, one of the few people to have a computer in Sandveld, wrote an email which she sent to every single address she had on her list, and she also asked everyone on that list to pass the email on to everyone on their own address lists, so that we could get the message out to as many people as possible.

I wrote a letter and sent it to Silverleaf School and asked them to talk to the parents at that school about donating shoes which were still in good condition but too small for their kids.

The money started coming into Frances' office. There were envelopes with small amounts of cash, and there were some cheques and even some donations from London. And bags and bags of lovely, hardly-used shoes from the Silverleaf parents.

Frances opened a special bank account for Two Bare Feet and we were up and running.

* * *

Our next step wasn't that easy, because we knew that all the children would want shoes (who wouldn't?) but we now had to decide who would and who wouldn't get shoes. For that, we had to rely on Frances, because she knew which families were the most needy.

We also had to make sure we got shoes that fit properly, because too many of our kids are wearing shoes that are hand-me-downs from an older sibling or cousin and which are either too big or too small. I thought that might be a good way to involve Irene, because she was learning some maths at school and she would be able to measure the children's feet and write down what size shoe they should have. I asked her to measure one child's feet so we could decide what size he needed, and I was shocked to see that she didn't know how to use a ruler. She thought you start measuring at one, because that is the first number. I had to show her that you start at zero, not one.

So Irene and I had a little discussion about measuring, using rulers and tape measures, and we talked about how you have to be careful to note that some tape measures have inches as well as centimetres, and you need to be sure you are using the same kind of measuring system each time. I would have loved to be in her classroom whenever her teacher next worked with them on measuring, and to see how many of the children in her class really understood what a ruler can do, the power it has. I knew that Irene would really know that now, because of her experience in measuring children's feet for new shoes.

The way we did it was this: Irene drew an outline of their feet on a page and wrote their names on the paper and measured the length with her ruler, and after work Patricia and I went to Pop Stores to buy the shoes. The shop assistant helped us convert the centimetres into a shoe size and we came back with three pairs of sturdy black school shoes.

The next day, I called a boy named Marius to come and sit with me while the other kids were playing outside. I said, "Marius, can you show me your shoes?" He picked up his foot for me to inspect. His shoe was completely cracked across the sole, and I could see his socks were wet. "Would you mind taking off your shoes, Marius?" I asked.

He took off his shoes and handed them to me. They fell apart in my hands. I was holding four pieces of shoes, rotten, wet, stinking. I took off his wet socks, and sent one of the kids to Frances to ask if she had a spare pair of socks somewhere, which she did.

And then I put the new shoes on Marius' feet.

He stood up. He was scared to walk in them, they were so shiny, so perfect. "Walk, Marius," I said, "You can walk in them, they are yours."

He took one step, then another. He was bent almost double, wanting to look at his shoes as he walked. And then he took another step, still gazing in amazement at the shoes, and his head hit the wall because he wasn't looking where he was going. But he wasn't hurt, just surprised, and we had a good laugh, and I said, "You can go and play now", and he did.

* * *

Irene took on this project with gusto. I showed her we had to plan carefully so we wouldn't waste the money, so we had to first think about all the things that are important. We talked about it for a while and I asked her to get a piece of paper and to write down the most important things.

"We need to remember who got new shoes and who is still waiting for shoes," she said. "Also, how much money we got and how much money we spent."

So we made a spreadsheet, not on a computer because we didn't have one at the school but on a big sheet of paper made from two sheets stuck together, and she wrote headings for the columns (CHILD'S NAME, SHOE SIZE, DATE HE OR SHE GOT THE SHOES, STILL WAITING FOR SHOES, HOW MUCH IT COST) and drew lines carefully using a ruler to make rows and columns, and she was in charge of filling in the names and the information each time another child needed a pair of shoes.

Of course I helped her to spell words like 'shoes' and 'waiting' and I helped her work out how much money we had spent by showing her how to add up the rands and the cents, but in essence it was her own work, and her being responsible for keeping it up to date meant she was doing spelling and maths homework without even being aware of it.

And that's how we got Irene started with the skills she will need in the future when she gets a job, and I am absolutely sure this girl will one day be someone famous and will use her seriousness and thoughtfulness, not to mention her planning and organisation skills, to do great things.

***

The Two Bare Feet charity gave me more opportunities to talk to my class about how we can look at things and compare them. We compared Marius' old shoes with his new shoes and talked about how much better he felt with dry feet. We compared school shoes with sandals, and talked about why sandals are not good in the rain.

We also tiptoed into the two-year-olds' class to watch them napping under their new colourful blankets, and later I borrowed some of the blankets so we could compare their old blankets with the new ones, and also measure them and see how the old ones were a bit too small. I drew an outline of a child from that class on a big sheet of newspaper and put the picture on the mat so it would look like a small child lying down, and we compared this measurement to the length of one of the old blankets – smaller than the child – and then compared the length of a new blanket – the same size! So now the children would be covered and they would be warm.

Each of my children took turns trying to cover himself with a too-small blanket and noticing how his feet stuck out, and then with a new blanket. And we also compared the beauty of the new ones with the old dull blankets, and we talked about all the colours and patterns that Debbie had used in knitting the blankets.

We did more and more work on comparing. I got each child to go out and find two leaves (not easy because there are very few trees which survive the wind in Sandveld, but there were some weeds growing against the back wall and a little stunted tree which a kind person had planted out front). We compared the sizes of the two leaves, and learned to use words for describing size which were more precise than small and big: words like long and short, wide and narrow.

Then we compared the shapes of the leaves, and learned to use words like straight, curved, wavy and spiky. And then I got them drawing lines which were straight, or curved, or spiky. And we did leaf imprints, using wax crayons and a page laid over the leaf.

We talked about colours and compared the different shades of green, light green and dark green, as well as the patterns on the leaves, if they had spots or stripes. And then each child stuck his leaf imprints on a piece of card and I hung them up on the wall so we could remember the words we had used to compare the leaves.

To get Irene working on comparing, I asked her to help me decide which would be the best kind of shoes to buy for Two Bare Feet and we talked about the different kinds of shoes, school shoes or trainers or canvas shoes.

This meant she had to think of criteria for comparing the different types of shoe, which was a lot more complicated than comparing the colour and size of a leaf. She came up with the idea of the shoes needing to be waterproof, and thought that canvas shoes would be unsuitable in winter because they would let the rain in. I loved seeing how she was really getting the hang of this kind of creative problem-solving. I asked her to think some more, and to give me more ideas about which shoes it would be best to buy, because sometimes the first answer is not the very best one and we need to think some more.

It took her a day to come up with the next criterion for choosing shoes: how hard or easy it would be for a young child to put on the shoes by himself, without help. She thought that laces would be too hard and that we should go for shoes with a Velcro fastening, because teachers are too busy to put on the shoes of every single child.

And what did I, Dolores, compare? I compared the Irene of that day, a person who could think independently and solve problems, as well as read and spell, with the Irene I had first met, struggling to read.

I compared my old style of teaching with my new teaching style: it seemed so different now that I knew something about Cognitive Education. My kids seemed to have woken up, to be taking an interest in the world around them, to be asking more questions.

I compared my workload now to what it had been before I had Annetjie's help, when I was in sole charge of thirty-six children. I compared how Annetjie had been when I first saw her sitting on the pavement outside the school waiting to pick up Devlyn to how she was now, growing into the job and showing more confidence with each day.

And I compared the Devlyn of before with the Devlyn I saw now. He was changing, he was learning to listen, and he was beginning to participate in group activities and to sing along to some of our songs.

CHAPTER TWENTY

We all know that when you are short of money you don't have much choice about what food to buy for your kids – you buy what you can afford. But we did notice that our kids were starting to come to school with snacks which may have been quite tasty and also really cheap, but which did nothing for their health. Some of these snacks were crunchy, crisp-like things full of salt and coloured bright pink or yellow. Others were sugary snacks like cereal. Reading the labels on these things was like going to a chemistry class. And I knew that that yellow colouring could not be good for anyone.

So Frances asked around and found someone, a nutritionist, who was willing to come and talk to our parents, at no charge, about healthy food.

It sounds easy, and it sounds like a good idea, but it has never been easy to get our parents to come to the school. Firstly, many of them are busy at work and don't have time, and in the evening they are reluctant, after a hard day's work, to go out again. But the other thing is that many of them are quite fearful when called to the school. They remember their own school days – a parent being called in meant you were in trouble! And the whole idea of having a White professional person telling them what to feed their kids made me feel (although I was surprised to notice this in myself, surely I should have got over this by now?) that once again White people were meddling in the most personal aspects of their lives, and it all brought back uneasy memories.

So Frances and Patricia put on their thinking caps. How could we get the parents to come to a meeting and to go away feeling like they'd had a good time as well as having got some really helpful advice? We wanted them to leave feeling happy and supported – in fact, to feel as happy and supported as we made their kids feel, day after day.

Patricia called in her army of helpful advisers and one of them knew a singer who was willing to come and entertain the parents, and we got some juice and fruit donated so the parents could have a snack, and the nutritionist's talk was just a part of a pleasant evening where the parents could talk to each other informally and have a bit of a party.

What the nutritionist said was that all these starchy snacks may be delicious but they are not that healthy. It's not that they should be banned, just that kids fill up on those and are still short of protein and vitamins. Protein and vitamins are what make a person strong and healthy and able to concentrate and learn. And a cheap and easy way to get protein and vitamins is to eat brown bread with peanut butter. That is what she said parents should be buying and that is what they should give their kids for snacks.

Well, I don't know how I felt about that, because these parents have so little money they just have to buy what they can afford, so that at least their kids are not hungry, and to ask them to buy special things is maybe asking a lot. But bread is something that is cheap here, and it is something they always buy anyway, so just choosing brown instead of white bread and adding peanut butter may be not such an expensive thing to do.

And I liked the way it tied in with my theme of comparison: more healthy or less healthy, cheap or expensive, delicious but not healthy, delicious but also healthy.

* * *

Annetjie was paid to work at Sunbeams for four hours each day. That was all the school could afford to pay her. So she would arrive at 8 o'clock, with Devlyn, having left the baby with someone whom Frances recommended, and stay till noon. Then she would say goodbye to all the kids and to Devlyn, and leave. It didn't occur to me to wonder where she went. I was too busy to even think of anything other than the kids in my class and what had to be done each day, but Frances called me one day and told me to look out of her office window. And there was Annetjie, sitting on the pavement outside the school, with her baby in her arms, waiting for the school day to be over at 2 o'clock so she could pick up Devlyn.

Well, sitting on the pavement is not such an unusual thing to do in South Africa, thousands of people do it. If you live in a township which is hours of travel away from your job, or from shops, you will not go back home every time you finish an errand, you will spend time sitting on the pavement. But I felt sad for Annetjie, sitting there. She looked so heartbreakingly vulnerable, so young, so small and alone.

One day Frances looked out of the window and Annetjie wasn't there. She got worried: Annetjie had disappeared once before as I am sure you remember.

So she went out to look up and down the street and Annetjie was nowhere to be seen. Frances walked down to the library to ask Patricia if she had by any chance seen Annetjie, and who should Frances meet in the library but Annetjie.

Patricia, never one to hold back, had seen Annetjie sitting on the pavement and asked if she wanted to come with her to the library, to look around and maybe to help her when it got busy, precisely between noon and 2.00, when she had finished working at Sunbeams and was waiting for Devlyn to finish his school day. This was a time when many older people wandered into the library, to sit in a calm quiet space and look at pictures in magazines, even though most of them couldn't read. So Patricia suggested to Annetjie that she could be there to welcome them and to show them the different magazines, and to keep it all tidy and put the magazines in tidy piles when people were finished looking at them, and to keep sweeping the front step because the sand was forever blowing into the library.

So Annetjie started helping out, without pay, just to keep busy and to have somewhere to be instead of sitting on the pavement. She worked with her baby tied on her back with a blanket, like so many women in Africa. She wiped the shelves, she swept the floor, and she watered the two miserable plants outside the door, which were withering in the blasts of wind and sand.

It was ironic, her working in a library, because she herself couldn't read or write, but Patricia is such a sensitive person and you could see that she made Annetjie feel needed and valued, and proud of how nice the library was looking now that she was in charge of keeping it tidy. Annetjie used her initiative to find a discarded bottle with a spray nozzle and to spray some water onto the path leading to the library so that the sand would be less likely to blow through the open door, and she was careful to spray just enough water to keep the sand down but not so much that it would make mud.

***

I haven't told you enough about Patricia. She is such a special person. I mean, all the people I am telling you about in this story about Sandveld are extraordinary in their way, they live in such difficult conditions and they do such wonderful work, they are so strong and so capable. But Patricia is something else.

To see her you wouldn't think that she was anything special. She is tiny, at least a head shorter than anyone else, in fact the same height as many of the children who are always surrounding her.

But wait until she turns her gaze onto you. She has this way of electrifying the people she speaks to. She gives off this amazing energy and warmth and enthusiasm. She is like a kettle bubbling over.

Patricia started the library from nothing, just an idea and the promise of an old shipping container. One of the donors from London gave the Trust some money to buy the container and also to paint it bright yellow, and he put some money towards buying basic shelving and a desk. Patricia then set about finding books.

When Patricia asks for something she has a way of making you really want to give it to her. Her first books were an encyclopaedia with a few volumes missing, but Patricia said, something is better than nothing! She got some other reference books too, because the librarian at the municipal library thought they were out of date but Patricia knew they still had some valuable information. And as time went by and more and more information was available on the internet, and reference books seemed to go out of fashion, so people would phone Patricia to offer her books from other libraries.

With all her contacts, and her persuasive personality, she got shipments of books from overseas and books being given away by parents from schools outside Sandveld. And a year after Patricia started to work in the library a grand opening ceremony was held with the funders from London, and the Trust also invited the then speaker of Parliament, who told us that she had never heard of Sandveld until she was invited by Patricia to the opening!

Two years later a permanent building was put up next to the container and an interleading door was created, so the library now had a lot of space which Patricia could use for meetings and for adult education too. That extra space was used as an office for processing the applicants for the new houses when the 1600 houses were being built, and later, when the housing issue was done, Patricia used the space to set up a support group for people who had HIV/ AIDS, so that they could meet each other and invite speakers on nutrition and health. She set up a chess club and found a retired teacher to come once a week and teach chess to any child who was interested. One of her most generous volunteers donated money to create a paved area outside the library made of alternating black and white tiles, so that life-size chess games could be played.

You can see that Patricia and her assistant Janice have over the years made this library into something much more than a place to find books. They are there every day, after school, and kids drift in asking for help with homework, or just to find a welcoming place to spend a few hours while their parents are still at work. Our houses are often so overcrowded, with so little space, that most kids don't have a quiet place to do homework, and in the library with Patricia and Janice they find not only space and quiet but also encouragement and praise for their efforts.

Patricia has also set up a teenagers' club and the teenagers often come and help out with activities for the younger kids over the holidays. Each year, for the weekend before Christmas, Patricia takes some of the most deprived kids on a camping trip. The kids she chooses for these trips are those who have never been outside Sandveld and have never experienced the fun of a weekend away with friends, in a safe place, with good food and lots of sports and singing and laughter.

Patricia is determined that 'her' library will never be a place where the books wait to be read and librarians wait passively for someone to come in, but rather a place where she can reach out actively to the community and invite them in, and provide for them what they don't have because they live in a place of such deprivation. "I just pull them in!" she said to me, when I once asked her how she did it. "I just pull them!"

And now she had reached out to Annetjie, given her something to do which had purpose and meaning, and at the same time added to her own staff a person of such grace and beauty and gentleness that I was sure there would now be more library visitors than ever.

***

I was still working with Irene on the reading programme. She was the most delightful student, because no matter what I gave her, she always took it seriously and went off and practised and by our next session she would have mastered that letter combination so that she could both read it and spell it.

I noticed that Isaac seemed to be hanging around us whenever I taught Irene. As I told you, Irene and I usually had our reading sessions just outside the classroom while my kids were having their nap, and perhaps Isaac, being that little bit older, didn't need a midday nap. So I invited him to sit with us, and honestly, I didn't plan to teach him reading, because of our decision to keep him in the younger group while he was still having so many hospital stays and not to overload him with learning while he was going through so much trauma, but he wanted it. He wanted to see what Irene was doing and he wanted to try it out. So I copied Irene's reading programme and made a set of letters and pictures just for him, and even though I didn't have time to work with him on his own, as I would have liked to, somehow we managed, Irene and I, to help him to recognise and even write letters, and to know their sounds. We had an interesting bit of discussion about comparing, my current favourite topic, because he was confusing 'b' and 'd', which Irene had done too earlier on, and so we talked about them facing in different directions, and we could compare directions of other things such as which direction a car was driving, and which direction the wind was blowing when it blew sand right into our classroom.

For Irene I suppose it was a way to revise everything she had already learned, but I think it also gave her a lot of confidence, acting the role of the teacher, and you could see she took to it. Perhaps she had in mind one of her own schoolteachers because she had some lovely little mannerisms when explaining something to Isaac. She would tilt her head to the side, put on a gentle little voice, quite different from her usual confident voice, and ever so carefully provide explanations and reminders, and tell him to try again.

And so it was that Isaac started to read the little books which the reading programme volunteer had given us.

Why I wanted to tell you about this is that it's not just about what Irene and I taught Isaac, it's about what he taught us. So what did Isaac teach us? He taught us that our pity for him was completely misguided, and that if you expect more of a child you will find that they expect more for themselves.

I loved the idea that in his future hospital stays, and there would probably still be several, he would be able to pick up a book and read to himself and his time would be filled with words and language and stories, instead of lying there alone waiting for someone to visit him.

CHAPTER TWENTY~ONE

I set up a game for my children, where they had to search in a specific patch of the playground sand for little plastic animals which I had buried. I defined the area by putting string around the designated patch, like archaeologists do, because our whole playground, as I told you, is nothing but sand, and I couldn't expect them to dig up all the sand, it would take months.

The fun part was searching, because they could use the spades we had stored (in our newly organised way!) and we had a little discussion about how to divide up the spades so everyone got a turn: we only had eight spades and thirty-six children. We borrowed one spade from another class to make nine, so that each group of four children had a spade (and how I hoped Louise would pop in at precisely that moment to see me linking our maths work to real life outside the classroom!).

We then talked about how, in each group of four children, each person would get a fair chance at using a spade, by waiting their turn. I secretly held back a few plastic animals in case they all got found by the first child and there would be nothing left for the others. It takes a lot of engineering and forward planning when you have so many kids in a class.

Anyway, the kids loved the game and found all the animals, and the next part of the game was to brush off the sand, bring the toys inside, and put them on the mat to sort them into groups. The toys we had were animals like elephants and lions, and some birds (ducks and penguins and an ostrich), and some swimming animals like sharks and fish and octopus, and some insects.

The digging itself was a fun game for the kids, but the best part for me was that it led to lots of talk and discussion, because after they had sorted all the animals into the three groups which I suggested (does it walk, fly or swim?) we talked some more about whether three groups were enough, or whether we needed more groups: for example, where do we put those animals who could do more than one thing, like both walk and swim, like elephants and people? Or walk and jump, like grasshoppers?

Of course, we could have divided the toys into biological classes – mammals, fish, birds, insects. That, I thought, was a bit beyond the level of my four-year-olds, so I kept it in mind for a later date.

We had come a long way from our early days of just learning the names of things. Now we had to learn to decide which items belonged in which group, and what to call the group. So that meant learning more words: the words for the items and the words for the group they belonged to. And each time we created a new group, it meant remembering the criteria we had used to define that group.

For the older and more advanced children in my class, I also wanted them to be able to use words to define the groups, to say what the characteristics of each group were, so that we could know for sure what belonged where. We defined birds as things with a beak and feathers, so we knew which ones went in the bird group, but then we needed an extra group for the different kinds of birds, because some can walk as well as fly, like the *mossies* (who always made me think of Devlyn); some, like the penguins at Boulders Beach, can walk and swim but can't fly; and some can do all three, they can walk and swim and fly, like cormorants and seagulls, which we often saw when we went to the beach.

It was amazing to see how, slowly, the children started to realise that you need some overlapping categories. "But Miss, we can't put the elephant here, in the walking group, because I saw in that book, elephants can swim! And we can't put them in the swimming group, Miss, because, Miss, that group is for animals that can only swim, like a fish, but elephants can do both! And anyway, Miss, you didn't talk about jumping, because a horse can jump, and a frog can jump, so what group do we put those in?"

This is how children talk in our schools. They call me 'Miss' and they say my name, 'Miss, Miss, Miss', over and over when they are excited, and I just love it.

We got into discussions, with my older kids, and with Isaac of course, about whether a penguin should be called a bird at all if it can't fly. They were using phrases like "you have to say what is a bird and what isn't a bird" and "we need to think about it some more" (that was Isaac, of course). I taught them a bit of logic: if only birds have feathers, and a penguin has feathers, then penguins are birds.

And so it was that my class started to learn about overlapping groups, Venn diagrams, which believe me is not usual for any kid age four, but certainly not for kids in our township schools who sometimes can't even count to ten before they start actual schooling.

I was so proud of them. These kids, who everyone was saying were unable to learn because of their poverty and because of living in violence and because their parents couldn't read and because... well, I won't repeat all those theories about why our kids don't do well at school, the main thing is that these little four-year-olds were thinking for themselves, using the kind of language I had never heard in a group of children that young, and having the kind of intellectual discussion I don't think you would hear at many other preschools.

***

Telling you about the kids digging in the sand to find the buried toys reminds me to tell you about some digging that happened not long ago on the other side of town, near the Cape Town business district. This is another story I have to tell you, because I think it will help you to understand some things that are very important to us here.

On the other side of town, near the docks, is an area which in the old days, maybe two hundred years ago, wasn't even part of the official boundaries of Cape Town. Now it has become a very busy place, where there are banks and fancy flats and shops. It is very near the new Waterfront development at the old docks, with all those expensive shopping centres and hotels and cinemas and restaurants.

I think that most people, our people anyway, always knew that under that ground were bodies. It was a paupers' burial ground a few hundred years ago, before Cape Town started expanding in every direction. The people buried there were the poor and the lonely: those who had no family, or whose families didn't have money for a proper funeral, or unidentified sailors who had drowned in shipwrecks, and slaves and indigenous Khoi-San people who had died far away from family who would have buried them in their traditional proper way.

So anyway, a developer bought a piece of land there to put up a huge building with shops and luxury flats which would cost millions of rands to buy, and sure enough, as soon as they started to dig for the foundations, his builders started to dig up bones. So the officials stopped the digging and the archaeologists were called in, and they started exhuming bodies to study them.

Well, that sounds sensible, doesn't it?

The only problem was, that our Coloured people realised that some of those bones were the bones of our own people, maybe even some of our great-grandparents, who knows. And it seemed to us that our ancestors' bones were being used for archaeologists to practise their science, and that the bones were being moved away so that the developer would be able to continue his money-making plans, and once again, our people were being forcibly removed from their little bit of sand.

I don't know how much you know about how our people were 'relocated', moved forcibly from our homes, after the apartheid Government passed the different forced removals laws. The Group Areas Act, which aimed to have each race group live in their own separate space, meant that over three-quarters of a million people, Blacks and Indians and Coloureds, were forcibly removed from their homes and towns and sent to live elsewhere. They were moved to badly-built homes, far from their work and often at higher rentals than where they had lived before. And as I have told you already, it meant that communities were uprooted and split up and people lost their friends and neighbours and extended family ties.

It is ironic, really, and the irony is not lost on me, that while I am teaching my kids to sort things into groups and categories, that is precisely what the apartheid Government did to us, to Coloureds and Indians and Blacks and Chinese people. We were sorted into categories and, believe me, there were no Venn diagrams; you could go to jail if you crossed a line, and overlapping a category was one of the worst sins you could commit.

So it was that thousands of Coloured people were moved to the Cape Flats. I don't know if you have been to Mannenberg, and Mitchell's Plein, but the Cape Flats is a place where nobody in their right minds would put houses, because it is an old flood plain, with nothing but wind and sand and winter floods.

People need roots. For some people, even if they don't have land or houses, they find their roots in their history, in the memories of the people they sprang from. But we Coloureds usually don't know which people we come from, because we are from mixed ancestry and don't know which of our ancestors were slaves or even where they came from, and which were Black and which were White and which were Khoi-San and what their story was. So we couldn't find roots in the history of our people.

But we could find some kinds of roots in the places we lived and in our communities. We did have a few places which we felt were ours to live in and District

Six was one of them, where we had created what came to feel like a kind of homeland for us. We had a community, we had our friends and neighbourhood support systems, and our own language, a mix of English and Afrikaans. And we lived at peace, Muslims and Christians, Coloured people and Black people and newly arrived foreigners like Greeks and Jews, all as neighbours.

And then we were moved and we lost those places. And now even our ancestors were losing their places because they were being moved out of their graves.

Well, to cut a long story short, there were protest meetings, and placards, and tempers flared, and believe me it was heartbreaking.

And in the end, which was no surprise for us Coloureds really, the Government decided to let the development go ahead, and the developer and the archaeologists exhumed all the bodies. The government is mainly Black, the developer and the archaeologists were mostly White, and as usual nobody was listening to the voice of the Coloured people.

I suppose there was a kind of compromise, because the bodies were respectfully reburied in a vault in a lovely stone memorial building; you can go and see it in Prestwich Street, you know, just down the road from here, and there are posters there which tell the whole story. And the whole place gives some kind of honour and recognition to all those slaves and Khoi-San and Black and Coloured people who laboured on the underside of the city and who never had marked graves.

It made me think, I can tell you. Because even though we will never know who each person was, we will never know their names, or how they lived their lives and how they died, I felt that they spoke to us from the sand.

And maybe all that stuff about categorising that I am teaching my kids, maybe that is all very well for education, but it has its limitations, and sometimes being too obsessed with categories and groups is a bad thing. Maybe that is what they were telling us, these voices from the sand. Because what we saw, when we looked at the photographs of the dig, was that all the bones were the same colour.

CHAPTER TWENTY-TWO

We had some discussions at university about how we can become better teachers if we know something about the child's home life. Louise thought, and I think I agree with her, that teaching is not something you can do in the classroom only; you have to think about the child's family and home, and what that family feels about education and school, to know how to teach a child in a way which he will be able to relate to.

What did I know about the lives of the children in my class? Of course, I now knew a lot about Devlyn and his mother, and their history. I also knew quite a lot about Isaac, because his special medical problems had led to his mother and I having lots of discussions, and I knew through talking to Rhoda, the volunteer who was looking after Isaac and his family, how he was doing when he was in hospital because she went to see him every day or so and kept us up to date.

I also knew a lot about Irene because of my friendship with Charlene, and even though she wasn't one of the children in my class, I was now helping her with homework on a regular basis, so I saw myself in a way as her teacher too, not just as a family friend.

And then Louise surprised us, because she suddenly said, "Well, you are all my students, and what do I know about you? Nothing!"

This was, of course, her way of leading up to her next assignment: we had to write about ourselves, our families, where we live, and why we wanted to be teachers. And we had to look to the past and the future too, because, as our lecturers had been saying over and over, organised thinking relates to time: thinking about the past and the future can help you to make sense of the present, and knowing about the past, and where you come from, helps you to know your identity. "If you know where you come from, it helps you to know who you are. And then I can learn who you are, too!"

So we were given this life history project: to find out as much as we could about our family of origin – parents, grandparents, and further back if possible – and write about whether we thought this had anything to do with how we lived now, and whether our lives now were defined by the past, by slavery and apartheid and all the things that had happened in this country, and whether we could move away from our history and make our lives into anything we wanted.

I looked around me, at my fellow students. About two-thirds of them were Coloured, two people in our class were White, and the rest of the class were Black. I suddenly envied them. They knew who they were: Xhosa, or Zulu, or Malawian, or Somali. I had an idea also that those who came from the Eastern Cape, whose lives had been less disrupted by their parents' migration from a country life to an urban life, would also know the entire kinship structure on both sides of their family, their mother's family as well as their father's.

And here we were, the Coloureds, with the most varied ancestry but also the most unknown. Very few of us had records with the names of past generations.

How on earth would we find out where we came from, who were those slaves in our distant past, who was that White man or that Khoi-San woman who would have been my great-grandfather or great-great-grandmother?

I had a lot of searching to do and suddenly I felt anew the loss of Grandma, who might have been able to fill me in on some of the facts. I knew that if I had asked her she would have impatiently told me to stop dreaming about the past and to do my homework, but if I had nagged a bit she might have told me something about our family. I thought of asking my mother, but her memory was so unreliable these days, sometimes I wasn't even sure if she recognised me. I asked Eddie, you remember, my cousin who got shot in the protest march when I was a child, but he didn't know anything and didn't care either.

The more I thought about it, the more confused I became. Surely, if this information was now lost to me, it couldn't make any difference to me whether some people in my family were once slaves, or whether they were Khoi-San herders or hunter-gatherers? Maybe they were, maybe they weren't. But on the other hand, the more recent story about how my community had been dispossessed of their homes and businesses and neighbours did matter to me and did affect how I responded when I saw how the kids in my class lived in poverty and didn't have spacious homes or gardens to play in, while the kids at Silverleaf School had swimming pools and trees and grass. So it did matter. It mattered a lot.

I noticed that I was comparing the life of the children at Silverleaf to that of my kids in Sandveld, and I didn't like myself for doing it, and I could just hear Grandma saying, "Dolores! Stop looking at everyone else and look at what you have!" But I knew that it was not just poverty which was affecting my children, but also the dispossessions, the brutality, the loss of their grandparents' homes and way of life which had been so completely shattered by apartheid. I wondered whether the children at Silverleaf, and their teachers too for that matter, whose parents and grandparents must have had such stable and safe lives, could even begin to understand the level of loss which our Black communities had known.

I spent the weekend reading in the Cape Town municipal library about the history of our people, the Cape Coloureds.

And this is what I found out: nothing new.

We are the descendants of Indonesian slaves and Khoi-San people and the early Dutch settlers and English farmers and Xhosa people. And who was where and when, and how things happened to my own family, can only be a matter of guesswork because no records were kept and nobody knows. All I can know for sure is who I am now, where I live now, what I do, and what I learned from living with those people in my family, the people I grew up with: Grandma Rachael, my mother for a few short years, and my uncles and the neighbours whom I haven't seen for so long.

I was stumped. We were supposed to present Louise with a rough outline for our project a week later, and I couldn't write a single thing. Some of the research I read was written by people who were determined to find their links to the past, to the first citizens of the Cape. Others were determined to move away from the apartheid-style divisions and towards a more unified Black South African identity. I kept veering from one point of view to the next, depending on what I was reading at the time and which opinion those writers held.

Louise, it turned out, was not at all surprised that I hadn't been able to write a single sentence, and that I had not a single idea about what I wanted to say. "That is where your training in Cognitive Education can help you out!" she said. "You have a problem, what thinking skills can you use to solve this problem?"

And she used our assignment, and the difficulties some of us were having with it, to teach us the three basic principles of how this kind of method works: the three main principles of what they call 'Mediated Learning', which is so different from regular teaching. The three main principles are things we need to make sure we include in every lesson we teach, but now we were thinking about them in terms of the lessons we ourselves wanted to learn about our own lives.

The first principle is 'intentionality'. I think I already told you about this, it is why I wrote all those hopscotch posters and put them next to Frances' office: so everyone would know what my intention was in teaching the kids to play hopscotch. And also when I explained to the class why I used a timetable, and tried to give my kids a window into my mind so they could understand what kind of thoughts I had while I was deciding what to do, in what order, during our day.

So for this assignment about our families and our identity, Louise wanted us first to think about our intention, what it was we were trying to do. I suppose my intention could be to decide how important it was to me personally that I couldn't find any information at all about my own family. But at the same time I had a lot of knowledge now about the history of my community. What did I intend to do with that knowledge? And for that matter, what was Louise's intention in giving me an assignment such as this? What did she really want me to find out about myself?

The second important thing is 'meaning': what is the importance, the meaning, of what you are trying to do? How will it make you feel if you find out something you didn't know about your family history? Or if you find out something about your family which is shameful, or ugly, or tragic? What will it mean to you if you find out nothing at all? For myself, I suppose the question was, how can you find some meaning in the history of your community, if you have no information about your own family's past?

The other aspect of making something meaningful, according to Cognitive Education, is letting your emotions into your learning and into your teaching. It's not just about efficient thinking skills. And to help my children feel something when they are learning, that meant letting go of the formal behaviour some people expect of a teacher and allowing myself to show my enthusiasm about our art project and letting the kids see my excitement about the changes happening to them. And my excitement should show my children that learning can be fun, and that there are new ways to think about things that are exciting and important.

And hopefully, even if they forgot all the letters and sounds and numbers, the one thing they would never forget was how excited a person can be when he learns something new.

And the third thing to always include in teaching, according to this theory about Mediated Learning, is 'transcendence'. For the children we teach, this relates to how we help them take what they have learned in the classroom and make it important and relevant for their lives outside that particular lesson and outside school, relevant to their lives with their families and their friends. To use the new skills when they go shopping or catch a bus or, later, make decisions about jobs and lifestyle.

For my own history project, transcendence would have to be about how I could go beyond my own personal story, perhaps to connect the story of my community with the stories of slavery around the world, or thinking about how being dispossessed affects the soul of a nation, not just here in South Africa but anywhere in the world. It could mean thinking about how poverty and violence affect children in other countries where, even if apartheid did not exist, they have had disasters of their own.

And, of course, a final step in this transcendence idea would be for me to think about how I live with what I have discovered. It would mean that I would need to find a way to recognise the loss I felt at knowing nothing about my family, at having no family tree, no ancient roots in any particular place, and to get over it, to transcend that loss, as Louise would put it, by knowing who I am now, by defining my identity in another way altogether.

And to take it a step further, I think maybe knowing what we have lost and how it has affected us can help us as teachers to make sure that the children we work with don't have that same loss. Somehow we have to try to give them a sense of identity, of who they are and where they belong, so they don't go blowing around the world like grains of sand in the wind.

CHAPTER TWENTY~THREE

Isaac came back after another operation and a week-long stay in hospital. He seemed quieter, which was hardly surprising, and he didn't want to go outside and play at break time, and we were quite pleased about that because he now had bandages on his hand again as well as on his head and we didn't want him to get sand in his wounds. Especially since a flock of goats had got into the school again and relieved themselves in the sand of our playground and we were worried about kids getting infections from the sand.

I wondered how his stay at the hospital had been for him: I knew his mother had been there every single day, after work, and that Rhoda had gone in every afternoon to read to him and to bring him some toys, and we had sent him some beginner reading books because he was now starting to read, but still there must have been long hours when he was just on his own with his pain and loneliness. So it was no surprise that it affected him, and our usually confident, talkative boy seemed a shadow of himself in his first week back.

While he was away, I had suggested to the class that we each make a drawing for Isaac, and put it into a book and send it to him with a 'get well soon' message. It was a good opportunity to get the children to think about what Isaac was going through, because even though they were still small, they knew that he had bandages and 'ouch' places on his body and I wanted them to remember him while he was away, and for him to know that we remembered him.

It took some organising, because I wrote out strips of paper saying 'Dear Isaac, Get Well Soon!' and I gave a strip to each child to include in his drawing. I first explained that the strip of paper would need some space, so if you draw all over your page, there will be no space for the paper. "So I want you, children, to first think, where will you put your message? And then plan your drawing so that you have space to glue the message."

Of course I could have got them to glue it on first, and then draw around it, but that would have been missing an opportunity to teach them some planning skills: to think about the space on the page, and how much space to leave, and to remember, even when you are enjoying your drawing, to still leave that space untouched. Well, most of them understood and planned their page, some of them didn't, but in the end I was pleased with how they were starting to learn to think about the space around them and to make sensible plans, and also I was really pleased when I bound all the pages together like a book. Martinus took a photo of the whole class and we stuck it on the front cover of the book, and I gave it to Rhoda to take to Isaac in hospital so that he would know we were thinking of him.

* * *

A few weeks after Isaac got out of hospital, we went on a trip to Kirstenbosch Botanical Gardens. I wanted my class to see the botanical gardens, firstly because there are no gardens in Sandveld, just occasional small patches where people try to grow some corn, or tomatoes. I wanted to show them how gardens can be beautiful, and can give us space to run around on grass (not just in the sand), but I also wanted to show them something about planning a garden: to explain to them how the planners think about what to plant, and where to plant it.

It's a place I used to know well, because nearby, just down the road from the gardens, was a little suburb, called Protea Village, where Coloured people used to live.

Grandma Rachael had known some people who had lived there, and she used to tell me how she would catch a bus and go and sit with them in what felt like a much more sheltered place than Woodstock. It was then a small village, with fewer residents, so it was quieter than Woodstock, less urban, with less traffic and less noise and crime, and much, much less wind. I think I told you that Woodstock, where we lived, is always buffeted and blown by the gales coming over the mountain, and sometimes the endless wind and noise just got too much, and going somewhere which was sheltered from the wind was like going on a holiday.

The people who had lived in Protea Village had been shunted out about ten years before I was born, and nearly all their houses were demolished, with only the church and three stone cottages left, but sometimes Grandma took me there on a kind of pilgrimage: we would take a taxi and walk among the trees and sit next to the lovely stone church which those Coloured landowners, descendants of slaves, had built using stones from the nearby Liesbeek River. Not that Grandma was much of a churchgoer, but she understood, and made me feel, the holiness and the tragedy of that place.

After apartheid ended, some of the people who had been evicted registered land claims in Protea Village, and not long ago there was an amazing ceremony, arranged by the municipality of Cape Town, and the ownership of a piece of land was formally returned to some of the claimants and others were given compensation if their land was now part of the botanical gardens. It was in all the newspapers; maybe you read about it.

Before I took my class on the outing to the botanical gardens I thought long and hard, and had endless talks with Frances and with Lorraine on the Trust, about whether to say anything to the children about Protea Village and the people who had been evicted from that place, because that is a place of mixed feelings for me, of memories of being with Grandma and running around free in the forest, and breathing that wonderful clean mountain air, but also of the sadness which ran under each of our visits like an underground river. But we decided that our kids were just too young for all that, too young to understand the history, and what is more, so many of the kids in my class are now from other countries in Africa, and they all have their own histories which should also be told, and I didn't know where to start.

You may wonder how we managed to get a whole class to Kirstenbosch, and to pay the entrance fees, when our school can barely buy a full box of Lego. Well, there is a school nearby, it is also a school for poor kids but they have a bus (which is driven, often, by the headmaster, so determined is he to make sure that the kids who live far away can get to school every day) and they agreed to lend us their bus for a morning. I phoned Kirstenbosch and spoke to their education officer and explained who we were, and they not only gave us free entry for the whole morning for every single child as well as for two teachers, but also offered to provide a guide who would talk to the children about the plants and give them an activity to do which related to what they would be seeing.

And so it was that my class learned that organising and planning and arranging in groups is something that you do not only in Dolores' class, because your teacher says so, but outside the class, in other places too: you put all the plants that need lots of water in one place, so it is easy to water them all together with one tap and one hosepipe; you put the tall plants at the back and the small ones in front so people can see all the plants; and you can put in one group all the plants that can be used as medicines, so that when someone is sick you know where to find the plants you need.

We took photos of the kids getting on the bus, which in itself was a great occasion for them because many of them had never been outside Sandveld, and watching their faces as we drove through the more leafy suburbs of Cape Town, with trees lining the road and no sand to be seen, was something I won't forget easily.

The day before the trip I had asked each child to tell me what he hoped to see when we got there, and I wrote it down, and on the way back I asked each one to tell me what he liked best, and wrote that down too. That night I put all their comments and some photos in a folder and made a cover with a photograph of a protea on it, our national flower. I spent the rest of the week looking at the folder with them, remembering what we had done and seen and reading back to them what they had said, what each child had hoped for and what he saw, and that way I think I showed them something about time, about how we plan and hope, and then do something, and time goes by, and we can look back and remember what we did.

For Devlyn, this was quite difficult because he probably didn't really understand abstract words like 'hope' and 'remember', but he certainly seemed to be listening, so I think he was starting to understand that you can use language to talk about more than what is here-and-now: you can talk about past and future, and things in your imagination too.

And for the other kids, it opened up for them a longer time perspective than they usually talked about, so that must be a good thing, because I think it should help them to one day understand the meaning of the long stretch of time in the past, and what their families lived through, but also to look forward to a future which can be different.

* * *

Devlyn was really doing well. With Annetjie supervising the children while they were doing craft activities or puzzles, I could spend a bit more time with him in the quiet corner, just talking to him, and helping him to understand longer and longer sentences.

He could concentrate better, and could sit still for quite a while, either playing on his own or playing with me. I invented all kinds of little games, which I used for teaching him new words. I would put out a few little toys, perhaps a toy table and chair, and a toy dog and a car, and ask him to put the car under the table, or the dog on the chair. Then I would pretend that I was looking for the car, and ask him, Where's the car? Is it on the table? Is it in my pocket? Is it behind your back? And he would grin and giggle and point to the car, and I would pretend I hadn't noticed where he was pointing, and eventually he started to say "under" and "on" and then "under the table" and then, one day, a very happy day for me and for Annetjie, he said, "Miss, car is under the table, you not see it?"

***

What I was doing with my class during that period was teaching the children to organise information, helping them arrange it in a way which they could see and understand, and trying to show them how much it helped us when we were organised. I got the Trust to buy me a big sheet of flat metal, and I painted on it a big grid, with rows and columns. I bought from the hardware shop lots of different coloured magnet buttons and wrote out cards with the names of all thirty-six children in my class. I stuck the name cards across the top of the grid, one name in each column, and down the left side of the grid I wrote the days of the week, one in each row. So every day, when the children came in, they had to take a magnet button and put it under their name, making sure to use the row which was the correct one for that day of the week.

So it meant that each day we could count how many children were present, by counting the magnets, and we could talk about how many were absent, and maths and numbers started to make sense. I would ask the children to count how many were absent and to work out how many chairs we could take away from the tables so that everyone had a chair and there would be no empty chairs taking up space. And we could count how many children were present and I could send someone to tell Bertha how many oranges we needed for our snack on that day. But also, learning to use a grid with rows and columns was quite an achievement for my four-year-olds, because it is usually something you only learn in maths lessons at school, and it was not easy for them to think about the rows and the columns, to trace their fingers down the vertical lines and across the horizontal lines and to find the exact spot where the column with their name on it met up with the row for that day of the week.

Sadly, every time he had another operation Isaac was absent for many days, but the grid allowed us to see clearly when he had not been in school, and to talk about how many days he had missed, and how we missed him and hoped he would be back soon. The empty spaces on the chart made it very tangible to us what a gap we had in our lives when any child was missing.

So the kids were starting to organise not only the space around us, by tidying their toys away into the correct space, keeping Lego with Lego and puzzles with puzzles, but also to organise time. I don't know if you have thought about it, but time is one of the most abstract things to teach a child. You can teach them to organise toys in boxes, because you can see the toys and you can see what does not belong. You can teach them to organise pencils in one place and paint in another, because you can see them. But you can't see time.

* * *

I was now halfway through my course on Cognitive Education and loving every moment of it – except for the project on family history, which I was still finding impossible to write. My husband sensibly said, why agonise over it now, give it some time to find its own way into your head, just keep reading about things, and go and visit some of the places your family knew, and remember what Grandma Rachael always used to say to you: "*Los dit, my kind*!" Leave it alone for a while! So I did, hoping that an idea, or a feeling, or something, would organise its way into my head, the way I was helping my kids to organise space, and time, and their world. If it works for them, I thought, it has to work for me too.

* * *

At the end of the term, before the Easter break, we had a little staff party at Sunbeams, to celebrate. What was there to celebrate? Just that we had got through another term. And at the party we had a chance to talk about the good things, like the new classrooms, and the blankets Debbie had knitted, and our two new assistants being such a help.

Frances asked Annetjie to say something about how it felt being a teacher, but she was too shy to say anything. Then it was Charlene's turn.

What Charlene said was, "Before, I used to be nothing. Nothing! I would walk down the street and nobody knew me, nobody thought I was good for anything. Now, when the children see me walking, they call to me 'Hello, teacher!' and they wave at me. And I feel so proud, you know?"

END of PART TWO

PART THREE

Showing and Sharing

CHAPTER TWENTY-FOUR

The art project had been going on for a good few months. My children had come a long way, and had moved on from drawing round things, like oranges and wheels, and long things, like bananas and pencils, to drawing each other, and drawing the sea and the sand during our walks to the beach.

Patricia lent me books from the library and I showed the children paintings by famous artists. We spent two whole weeks talking about and looking at still life paintings, and together with Annetjie I set up still life groupings in the classroom for them to paint.

I showed them paintings of landscapes, and we went outside and looked at the mountain at different times of the day, to see how the light and the colours changed. It gave us a chance to keep on using comparison skills: which part of the mountain is higher, which bit is flatter, which part is more pointy? Look, the rocks look more blue now, when the sun is setting, and earlier, in the morning, they looked more orange.

So gradually we were building up a huge collection of the children's drawings, on all kinds of themes and subjects.

I was going to keep abstract painting for last, because I was scared that they would think it was just random movements of a brush, without really looking or thinking, the way they had been painting before we started the art project. I know that abstract painting is much more than that, but I didn't know how to explain it to them, or to anyone else for that matter.

But I also wanted to give them a chance to use different materials, so I added one session each week where the children were simply given a range of different kinds of paint and crayons, and whatever other materials we could lay our hands on. Patricia at the library was, as usual, a master at getting people to donate stuff. We had small pieces of coloured card, reject mosaic tiles from the factory nearby, glue and glitter and bits of coloured wool and ribbon.

And they just got on with making beautiful creative original things to look at, but now, instead of their just grabbing stuff and attaching it without even looking at what they were doing, they were choosing carefully, taking time to think about what it would look like, and – how wonderful! – telling their friends, "Look! Look what I did!" and running up to me when they were finished to make sure that I wrote their name on their picture.

* * *

Strangely, Irene and Annetjie took to spending time together. Some afternoons, once Annetjie's work at the library was done, she would come back to Sunbeams to pick up Devlyn, and instead of going straight home, she would stay for a while. If Irene had done her homework they would sit together.

It was strange. Annetjie was a teacher and a mother, and Irene a seven-year-old child. Although maybe not so strange. Annetjie looked so young, much younger than her twenty-something years, because she was so tiny and had such a child-like face and body. And Irene was mature beyond her years, perhaps too mature and serious for a child.

One day, as usual not minding my own business and curious to know what they were always talking about, I wandered over to say hello. And what should I see, but Irene teaching Annetjie to read.

It took my breath away. Irene herself had just mastered reading, with the help of the special reading programme, and here she was, handing it on to the next person who could use it.

I was really touched, because it made a kind of link between the volunteers, who were teaching reading to kids in the townships, and me, having been shown how to use the programme, and Irene, who was struggling at school, and now Annetjie, who had added so much to my classroom and whose lovely boy was now learning how to learn. It somehow closed the circle in a way which was unexpectedly joyful.

Talk about transcendence. The little effort I had made with Irene had grown beyond anything we expected. Maybe what they mean by transcendence is unexpected benefits. Maybe it means that all that effort we put into becoming better teachers, and to supporting people like Devlyn and Isaac and Irene, can lead to something that we didn't expect or even hope for. Like Annetjie learning to read.

***

Thinking about it later, and talking about it with Charlene, I started to see that Irene being able to do this said a lot about her own real generosity of spirit, which we all had seen a long time ago when we first met

Charlene and Irene and saw how they helped each other, almost like two friends instead of mother and daughter, and how Charlene could rely on Irene to be sensible, to do her homework, and to help around the house without being asked.

But it also linked in with something we had discussed in our tutorials at university, about the best kind of teaching being the kind that gives a student feelings of competence and confidence, and how that is almost more important than giving them knowledge about a topic, because when you feel competent it motivates you to want to learn more, and it allows you to take risks and even make mistakes and still carry on learning and never give up.

Of course, those people in Cognitive Education are never satisfied when you think you have finally understood something. So Louise had to explain to us that it's not enough to feel confident and competent in a general way. We have to also make the students aware of exactly *what it is* that they are competent at. They have to know not only that they can do something well, but also *how* they succeed in doing it well, what strategies they have used, what kind of thinking skills. That way, they will be able to use those cognitive skills again if something similar comes up in the future.

That feeling of competence that Irene now had, where she felt she knew enough of something to teach it to someone else, was precisely what Cognitive Education was about: knowing something, and *knowing that you know it*.

* * *

But something else was worrying me now. I could see, and so could the teacher in the classroom where

Charlene worked, that Charlene was not herself these days. She seemed to be moving more slowly, and to be smiling a bit less. I spoke to Frances, because she is so good at managing staff and anyway it wasn't really my business from a work point of view, though it was my business because Charlene was a friend.

Well, lots of people get sick here, and sometimes we don't know what it is, and sometimes it is AIDS. But when Charlene finally got to see a doctor, after waiting for eight hours in a queue, he sent her for X rays at the hospital and it turned out that she had TB.

***

A few days after Charlene told us that she was sick, and we were still trying to come to grips with it, Irene was sitting at my table doing her homework. Now and then she just stopped and sat there, thinking. I sat with her, not knowing if she wanted to speak, or what I should say.

Irene said, "You know, I think my Ma was always very strong. Even before she got sick, when my Pa didn't have work and then when he went away for a long time, and we didn't have a house, what did she do? She made herself tidy, put on her best hat, and held my hand tight, and she went to her madam where she worked, and she said, 'Madam, I turn to you. We need help. We need money for rent, I will pay you back, but we need to have a roof over our head.' I think another person would maybe feel too shy to say that, but my Ma, she does what she has to do. That's what she always says to me. You do what you have to do."

I didn't know what to say and I was scared that if I spoke Irene would see I was crying.

"And now", continued Irene, "what my Ma has to do is take her medicine to get better, and she needs to rest a lot, and not work so hard. And what I have to do now is to be strong, like her, not cry, and to keep on learning at school, and help clean the house."

* * *

One morning a few days later I was walking to work from the taxi rank and I came upon Frances, just standing outside the school grounds, in the street, and staring at the gate. My first thought was that someone had broken in again and stolen our equipment. But no, she was perfectly calm.

"Good morning, *skattie*, how are you?" she said. "Don't you think this wall is really ugly?"

I hadn't really noticed our outside wall, it was just part of the general landscape of Sandveld, functional and not pretty. But it served to keep the dogs and goats out, most of the time anyway, and the kids in.

The wall was a standard brick wall, painted white, although the white had long since given in to the abrasion of the sand in the Cape wind so most of the paint was scraped off and the brick was exposed in several places. Some of the bricks had started crumbling off the top of the wall and it looked like it wouldn't be long before that wall started reverting to its original material, and we would just have one more pile of sand in front of our school to add to all the piles of sand in our playground.

On the wall Martinus had painted a sign, a long time ago, saying 'SUNBEAMS CRÈCHE' and he had later tried to cover up the 'CRÈCHE' and write 'PRESCHOOL' when the Trust made the decision about making Sunbeams more educational. That in itself was a bit messy, but the worst part was that the last few letters of the word 'Preschool' were not in line with the rest of the word and were rising towards the top of the wall, making the outline of the word curve upwards, like a moon, like a banana, and not at all like the kind of writing that we hoped our kids would learn to do.

Perhaps it was Martinus expressing his creativity, but Frances and I would have preferred the sign to be in a straight line so that people could read it easily and so that it looked professional, like some of the signs you see on other schools outside our township.

The kids were arriving already so we had no time to talk more about the wall, but later, when the kids were eating lunch, I thought about it. What could we do? I asked Frances if Martinus could perhaps try to do some basic repairs on the wall. That would make it look less neglected, but not less ugly. Patricia came over from the library after work and we were talking to her about it.

"I know someone who could help!" she said, her face lighting up as it did every time she had a bright idea. "There is an artist, Peter, sometimes he helps out in the library, maybe he can help us."

I could see Patricia was almost jumping up and down with excitement. "I am going to visit Peter right now!" she said. "You can come with me if you want, or not, I am going!"

It must have been funny, watching her walking out and Frances and me following her. The walk to the village where Peter lives was quite long, but Patricia was marching along as if her feet didn't touch the ground. She knew where Peter lived, she had visited him before, and she knocked on the door, and though he was surprised to see three uninvited women on his doorstep he graciously invited us in.

The upshot of all this was that he agreed to come to Sunbeams one day, after Martinus had finished repairing the wall, hopefully on a day when it would not be windy (ha ha), to help decorate the wall with a huge mural. I explained to him what I had been doing in my class with the art project and he said nothing about creativity, in fact he liked my idea very much, and he said, "Well, why don't we give this job to the kids in your class, they are obviously ready for it! I'll help them."

Getting the paint was the next problem. Patricia again came to our rescue and called in one of 'her ladies'. Patricia has contacts who support the library and her various projects, and they manage to get donations of all kinds of things. She phoned Helen, a contact of hers who runs a stationery business.

Helen was thrilled about the wall project and said, "Just get Peter to phone me and tell me what kind of paint, how much, what colours, and I will get it delivered to you."

And so it was. One calm day, Frances checked the weather report and when we were relatively sure, or as sure as you can be in such a windy place, that the wind would be quiet that day, she phoned Peter and asked him if he could come. The paint was ready, the wall had been fixed, and by the end of the day our kids were covered in paint, but our wall was beautiful, covered with pictures of butterflies and trees and children and the sea and fish in purple and red and gold.

Martinus' sign still curved upwards because at the last minute, just as Peter was getting ready to paint over it and do the lettering in a straight line, we noticed Martinus standing there, watching us, and Frances said to Peter:

"Stop! Not the sign, we love our sign, please just leave it!"

So we have the most beautiful wall in Sandveld, with a crooked sign, and that is just right for us. Nothing around here is perfect anyway.

CHAPTER TWENTY-FIVE

Rhoda, the very kind lady who had been taking Isaac to the hospital for his appointments and had visited him there every single day, and was still supporting his mother and granny by bringing them food and warm clothes, started visiting us at Sunbeams after Isaac came out of hospital, just to see how he was doing in class.

So we sometimes sat, at break time, watching the kids in the playground and chatting about all sorts of things. She was interested in whether we would decide to move Isaac to the older class as he was already starting to read and write, but at the same time it was easy to see what lovely friendships Isaac had with some of the kids in my class, and we went back and forth, discussing what was more important, friendships or school advancement.

We both thought that for Isaac particularly, with his scarring being so severe, perhaps being a bit older than the others would stand him in good stead later, at school, when you do need to be big and tough to cope with that onslaught of lots of older kids running wild in the playground. I just wanted to give him as much time as possible in the protection of our preschool, where we could watch him all day, making sure his bandages stayed clean and that he was safe and happy. Learning could, and would, come later – especially now that we knew there would be a local school and he would be able to walk safely to school every day from his house nearby.

Rhoda was also interested in Devlyn because she knew that he had become in some way my 'special project'. Of course, I know (before you say anything) that if you are a teacher you are not allowed to have any favourites and that favouritism will affect all the other children badly, so I worked very hard to give all the children a lot of attention, but still, Devlyn had somehow smiled his way into my heart.

I was still perplexed by him. With all the teaching I had given him, with all the careful repetition of vocabulary, and showing him over and over what I expected him to do in class, he had made progress and was talking more. Initially, during circle time, when all the children would sit and listen and join in the singing, Devlyn would just get up and walk around, but now he would sit with everyone and even sing along. But he never volunteered to say anything, he never initiated an idea. He was still the child who, compared to all my other kids, was the most passive, and had the least ability to learn new things.

Rhoda had by now got to know the Children's Hospital quite well, through her many visits with Isaac and her discussions with the staff there – not only the surgeons but the nutritionists and the physiotherapists and the occupational therapists. So she came up with an idea: to ask Devlyn's mother, Annetjie, if she would agree to bring Devlyn to the hospital, and to ask a few doctors and therapists to look at him, to try to see why he was still so small, why he couldn't learn like the others, why he could not concentrate.

Annetjie was, understandably, alarmed. "You mean he is sick? He got that sickness? That's why he's so small? No! I know it! He is not sick, how would he get that?"

She meant HIV/AIDS. We all know about this plague, some of the parents of our kids have it, although we don't talk about it because it is confidential and also because, in the early days when it started, it wasn't talked about at all. These days people can get medicines, and pregnant mothers can get medicines so they don't pass it on to their babies, but still, it crept and crawled and grew in our community in its silent, deadly way.

We hadn't for a moment thought that Devlyn had AIDS. I was thinking about malnutrition, because Annetjie had told me of her hard times when she was pregnant with Devlyn. Rhoda was thinking more on the lines of asking the occupational therapist and the speech therapist to advise on the kinds of activities and exercises we could do in the classroom to help children like Devlyn to concentrate, but she also wanted the nutritionist to give him a general check-up, to make sure he was eating the right things and to ask if he might be able to catch up on his growth now that his mother had proper housing, and a job, and could buy good food. We knew what we were feeding him at school but we didn't know what he was getting in the evening, or on weekends, or during the school holidays.

Last year, there was a research project carried out at Sunbeams and someone came and weighed all the kids once a month. She also made sure to weigh them on the last day before the long summer holidays and then on their first day back at school after the holidays. And what she showed us was shocking: during term time, while the kids were at school, they gained weight slowly, just like kids should do when they are eating well and growing. But after the long school holiday at least a third of them had actually lost weight. So they were not eating well during the holidays, when they were at home and not getting the food which we at Sunbeams could afford to give them.

That had led to some of our wonderful volunteers setting up a holiday feeding programme. They got donations of staple foods, rice, *samp* – you know, that dried corn – milk powder, peanut butter and dried fruit, and those tins of pilchards in tomato sauce, from the people shopping at supermarkets in more wealthy suburbs, and packaged the food so that each family got a big pack of food just before the Christmas holidays. Of course, the food packages would not be enough for a whole family for six weeks, but they would hopefully add some protein and vitamins to the kids' diet to tide them over.

Anyway, I am getting sidetracked, because I wanted to tell you about Devlyn's assessment at the hospital. I felt really bad at having upset Annetjie, just when she was getting to trust us and to feel secure in her work, and you could see she was blossoming. She smiled, there was a bounce in her step, and her baby, now eight months old, had stopped her listless crying and was sitting up and did not have a constantly runny nose. So we spent a lot of time explaining to Annetjie that we didn't think Devlyn was sick. We just wanted to help him, to help him to learn and grow.

"I am also small," said Annetjie. "All my family were small, my mother also." But when I told her that the other children in the class were growing now, and putting on weight, and Devlyn still stayed small and thin, she did start to think that maybe he needed more help. Also, she was in the classroom all day with us and she could see that he was not learning the way the others were. I told her she didn't have to decide now, but I did hope she would think about it.

Speech therapy and occupational therapy are services we have never had here in Sandveld. I know that the kids at Silverleaf do have this kind of help: they have a speech therapist, an occupational therapist and a physiotherapist at that school. Any teacher can ask their advice about a child at any time, and the therapists come into the classroom and give the teachers ideas to help their kids if they have any movement or coordination or speech or developmental problems.

Of course, it takes money. I asked the teachers at Silverleaf how it works. Who pays these people their salary? They told me that any parent who wants his child to have sessions with any of these therapists pays the therapist directly. This costs a lot of money, believe me; a few sessions of therapy would probably cost what someone in Sandveld would earn in a whole month. But that is not a problem in that community, they have the money in plenty.

The therapists gave the teachers lots of advice and training and help, and for that support neither the parents nor the school had to pay, because the school was providing these therapists with a place to work for which they did not have to pay rent.

But all that was an undreamed of luxury for us. And here was Rhoda, offering to pay with her own money for Devlyn to see some doctors, and for a nutritionist to advise Annetjie, and us, what we should be doing to make sure he was eating the right things. Who could turn down such an offer? So in the end, Annetjie agreed, and even became quite excited at the thought that her Devlyn would be getting all this help. She knew very well what a bad start he had had in life, we didn't have to tell her. And Annetjie had a very special thing about her: she was so resilient, and in spite of all the bad things that had happened to her she never seemed to feel sorry for herself. When she did tell me bits about her past life, she never seemed to be asking for sympathy.

So, a few weeks later, the appointments were arranged, and one morning Rhoda picked up Devlyn and Annetjie and the baby and Annetjie's big bag with nappies and bottles for the baby and a snack for Devlyn which Bertha provided, all nicely wrapped up, and off they went in her car. It was actually quite festive in a strange way, because even though he was going for a day of doctors' examinations and possibly some not-so-pleasant things like blood tests, we were really very excited to see one of our own getting the care and attention he needed. So while I was worried about what problems they might discover Devlyn had, I was also quite hopeful.

***

The doctors had asked Annetjie for permission to have Rhoda sit with them and take notes, because it was quite complicated and they were worried about how much Annetjie would understand and remember, since her English was not very good. They also sent me a questionnaire to fill in, which they said would help them to get the bigger picture about how Devlyn was at school.

Rhoda and Annetjie told me about it in detail the next day. Mainly, what the doctors had tried to do was find information about Devlyn's early years, starting with the pregnancy, when Annetjie herself hadn't had enough food. They explained how that can affect an unborn baby: it is as if the mother's body and the baby's body are in competition for the little bit of food there is, and that means that both of them suffer.

They thought that he had been born full term, because that is something Annetjie remembered, but she couldn't tell them what his birth weight was, because who ever heard of having a scale to weigh a baby, or someone to write things down, when you are so poor that you have your baby on your own, in a shack? And the birth weight would have been an important thing to know, because the doctors said that when a baby is born full term but has a low birth weight, those children sometimes have learning problems later on.

The doctors also asked Annetjie lots of questions about whether she had drunk lots of alcohol or taken drugs while she was pregnant, because those are also things that cause serious problems for children later on. The doctors told them that one of the things they were seeing recently was children who had brain damage because their mothers had been smoking *tik*. I don't know if you know about this drug, it is the cheapest and most addictive one and is used by such young kids, by the teenagers in their gangs, by men and by women. It is unbelievable what a scourge this has been in the Cape.

But Annetjie was adamant: she would never have done anything to harm her kids, she had never drunk alcohol or taken drugs. They asked if she had felt ill or felt well during the pregnancy, but she couldn't remember, because it was a time of such trauma and such fear and trying to just get through another day and stay alive that she didn't remember much about it. Rhoda gave the doctors the form I had filled in, with lots of questions about Devlyn's behaviour at school, and how he learned, and they now asked Annetjie the same questions.

The doctors spoke some more about malnutrition, and they did some tests and found that Devlyn as well as the baby had anaemia and needed lots more protein and iron and vitamins, and they explained how malnutrition can prevent a child from learning. Well, that at least was something we could do: we could make sure that Devlyn ate a bit more, and knowing Bertha as I do, I was sure she would put a little extra aside so that Devlyn had a bit more meat than the others. Rhoda, of course, offered to get some vitamin supplements and the doctors wrote down a prescription for her.

The doctors also told them about something they call a 'double hazard': a child living in poverty spends his time among people who are also lacking in food and are often ill, and so these children are exposed to more illnesses than children who do not live in poverty. And they are more likely to get an infection than a child who is well-fed, because poor kids don't have a well-developed immune system. So the illness then weakens their immune system even further, and then when they are again exposed to sickness they catch everything going around, and they are still not getting the proteins and vitamins they need to get stronger, and it goes on and on, in a vicious cycle.

It was a long day, with lots of tests being done and lots of questions.

The next week they had another meeting, after the doctors and therapists had had time to discuss everything and summarise what they had found. This time I had to go along because they said that they wanted to make sure that the school, where Devlyn spent most of his time during the week, would know what they had to say. Poor Frances, she had to take over my class all on her own while I spent three hours at the hospital.

Well, what they told us came as a relief, because it turned out that Devlyn had nothing major wrong with him, only some small problems. But it was a relief only at the beginning, because when they started to tell us all the small things, I could see how they added up to quite a big thing.

What the doctors and therapists thought was that Devlyn was showing signs of attention deficit and hyper-activity. They explained that it is something that they had seen in quite a lot of kids, and they were going to give me, as his teacher, some strategies to help. I asked about medication, because I had heard that in some cases the doctors can give medication for this, but they thought that his attention problems were not really severe enough for that, and that as he seemed to be improving since Annetjie moved from Overcome Heights, we should just keep on working with him and watching for further improvement, and come and see them in six months' time to talk about it again.

In addition, the doctors told us that he had glue ear in both ears, the result of long-term infection in his middle ears, and his hearing was not very good and he should have grommets, which is a tiny opening in the ear drum to let the ear drain and get back to normal. I was surprised to hear this, because Devlyn had had a hearing test when all the kids at school were tested and they said he could hear, but the doctors told us that middle ear problems are not constant, they change all the time, and a child can have completely blocked ears one month and the next month it clears up. But thinking about how his nose was always running, with thick green mucus, it did make sense that his ears were affected by that. So that explained why he would respond if you were close to him and spoke directly to him, but would often not seem to be listening when I was talking to the whole group. Well, that was something that could be fixed too!

They also spoke about malnutrition, and warned us to make sure he not only had enough protein and calcium, but also did exercise to build up his bones and muscles. Annetjie had to make sure he went to bed early and had a good night's sleep every night.

But then the psychologist who was part of the team spoke up, for the first time, and she gave us a long speech about the circumstances of Annetjie's life even before she had Devlyn, and how she had lived for years in fear, not knowing what would happen to her next, where her next meal would come from and whether she would have a roof over her head, not to mention the violence taking place around her and being done to her.

And the psychologist said, don't ever underestimate what stress like that does to people. It can affect an unborn baby too. It makes people more than usually geared up for danger, and makes them respond to things in certain ways. And it can certainly cause a little child like Devlyn to be someone who is filled with anxiety and to show the sort of watchful behaviour that I had noticed in him: looking around all the time, eyes swivelling in all directions, never settling down to do any one thing. She asked us to think about whether it would be likely that a person constantly on the watch for danger could ever let down his guard and listen to his teacher telling him about the ABC, or the weather. Or to look at the beauty of the sea and the mountains.

Well, it was a long and gruelling and anxious day, and we just felt so sad for Devlyn and for Annetjie, and the baby too, because they had been through so much, and so much damage had been done to them.

But in the end it was good. Because what that psychologist said was this: that in spite of all the things Annetjie and Devlyn had gone through, and in spite of the fact that Devlyn didn't have a good start in life and seemed to display some signs of attention deficit, there was research which showed that all of this can be overcome, if the child is looked after in the right kind of environment. And what she meant by the right kind of environment was this: that he was getting warm and stable care from his mother, or from someone who was always there, always able to take notice of his needs and to respond to them consistently. And now that they had adequate housing, a roof that didn't leak and a door to close against the outside and all the dangers out there, they could feel safe, and Annetjie was freed up to be what she was able to be: a really good mother to her kids.

And the other thing the psychologist said was something that made me feel proud of what we are doing at Sunbeams. She told us that there was some research that showed that children with malnutrition and learning problems related to poverty and extreme trauma can be helped by being given lots of conversation and stimulation and experience with toys and stories, and that these kids can then overcome the disadvantages of their environment and learn just like anyone else. And all of that was exactly what Sunbeams Preschool was giving to all our kids, not just Devlyn.

It just shows that even if your past includes things you would rather not have experienced, you can change the effect is has on you, and nobody needs to have something wrong with them forever just because of what happened to them in the past.

CHAPTER TWENTY-SIX

This whole long story that I have been telling you, about my work in Sunbeams and about Sandveld, and how our kids live today, is just a small part of the big story about South Africa and what has been happening here for nearly four hundred years since the Dutch East India Company, and later the British East India Company, decided to settle here in the Cape, and found that the local people already living here had different ideas from theirs about how to live their lives.

So my story is a little story within a big story, like those tins of chocolate drink powder we had when I was a child, tins which had a picture of a chocolate drink tin on them, and on that picture was another picture of another tin, and so on and on, getting smaller and smaller but still, recognisably, tins of chocolate.

But I want to tell you another story, a story which fits inside my little story of Sunbeams, and it is a story of a different kind, because it is a story about a storyteller.

Nicola is the storyteller I want to tell you about. You may think that I am going totally off track now, telling you one story after another, but this one is really important, because it involves Devlyn.

Nicola came to South Africa from the UK to listen to stories told by people in South Africa, because that is what she does – she collects stories from around the world, written stories and oral stories, and she tells her stories to other people, and helps other people to tell their stories too.

Most of the people she helps to become storytellers are adults who have learning difficulties. I don't know if you have thought about it, I know I didn't until I met Nicola: most people are not interested in listening to the stories told by people who have learning difficulties. Maybe most people assume that they have nothing interesting to tell us. But Nicola sees it differently and she has been collecting the stories of people who were kept in closed institutions in the UK for years, some of them all their lives, because they were strange, or different, or had learning difficulties. Now that those institutions have closed down, and these people are living in flats and houses, they can tell their stories, as long as there is someone who will listen.

And Nicola and her team are people who listen, and who help the rest of us to start listening too.

Anyway, Nicola came to Sandveld and offered to tell a story to my class. Of course, I was thrilled – what an opportunity, to have a world-class professional storyteller come to our little school!

The story she chose to tell us was a traditional African tale about a snake who threatens a village, and a brave man who talks to the snake and tells the snake to go away. She had rolled up a long green curtain to make the snake, and it was truly terrifying, at least three metres long, and flexible, so you could just imagine it as something alive and wriggling. It was interesting to see that even though they had seen her rolling up the curtain, some of the children were really scared of that snake because of the dramatic way she spoke about it.

She needed to choose some children to play different parts in the story, and asked me who I thought should play the different roles. Once we had chosen the minor roles, we had to choose the person who would play the brave hero.

"That's the one," I said, pointing at Devlyn. "He should be the hero."

Because Devlyn was so small, we worried that the children sitting at the back of the room would not see him over the heads of those children sitting in front, so we asked him if he would stand on a table, and when Nicola got to the part of the story where the brave man talked to the snake, Devlyn had to say to the snake, "Go away!"

"Do you want to do it, Devlyn?" I asked. I didn't want to frighten him, or to ask him to do something if he didn't quite understand what I was asking of him.

"Yes!" he said firmly. "I do it!"

And so it was that Devlyn, the smallest boy in the class, the one who I feared would blow away in the wind, became the strong man of the village, and stood on the table, proud and straight, and looked that snake right in the eye and said, "Go away, snake! You go away and don't come back!"

* * *

I think you can choose to look at things in two different ways: in the short run and in the long run. In the long run, I know that some of our kids may not make it. They may get sick, they may get into gangs and drugs, they may get shot or stabbed, or they may simply fail at school and never get a job and live on the fringes of society, starving and desperate. But it is also possible that because of the small things we have done here at Sunbeams, the 'short run' things like the art project, and learning to think and solve problems, they may grow up to be people who play a part in our community, and they may become the generation that is not lost but found.

So even though there is still so much to do in this country, so many big and important things like making sure there are jobs, and decent housing and water supplies, those are 'long run' things which a teacher can't do anything about except vote in the elections. But in the short run, in our own community and at our own schools, we can do the small things which make a difference.

And making it possible for Devlyn to stand there on a table, taking the main role in the story and feeling like a king, is the kind of short run thing which we can do.

* * *

Inspired by Nicola's storytelling session, I started to include storytelling in the classroom. I don't mean reading stories out loud; that is something we had always done. I mean helping the children to tell stories themselves.

At first it was hard, because they just didn't know what I wanted of them and couldn't seem to think of anything to say, and even when I suggested they tell a story about playing hopscotch, or about a toy car they liked to play with, they just couldn't think of anything.

To show them what I wanted, I made up little stories about simple things, things that happen every day at school, like a boy falling off a slide, or children digging in the sand and finding a lost toy. I drew simple line drawings, showing each event in the story on a separate card, and then lined up the cards, from left to right, in their correct order and talked about what happened first, and what happened next, and what happened in the end.

I would sit at a table with six children and give them a few props, maybe some cars and people and toy animals, and while they were playing with them I would tell them the story they were playing out. I became their voice. "One day, the lion drove in the car, and he met some people, and they said, 'Can I drive in the car with you?' And the lion said, 'No! Go away!' So the children were sad. And in the end the lion said, 'Okay, you can have a turn.' And the children said, 'Thank you, lion!'"

They were really simple stories, actually just describing what the kids were doing while I watched them play, but they gradually got the idea. After a few weeks of this, I would call out a name of a child and ask him if he wanted to tell me a story, and we would sit in the curtained-off quiet corner and he would tell me his story and I would write it down in exactly his own words, not changing anything even if his grammar was not so good, and later read it to the whole group.

And so we became a storytelling class, as well as a looking-and-drawing class.

* * *

Storytelling is something I grew up with. I remember how Grandma Rachael and my uncles would meet in our house in Woodstock, with some of their friends who had lived in District Six before they had been moved to the Cape Flats, and the conversation was always about the same thing. They used to reminisce about their lives before the expulsions from District Six and Simonstown. They talked for hours about how life was when they were still a community, in the good old days.

They had lost nearly everything, but they had kept their memories about those places and the lives they lived there. I heard those stories over and over, year after year, and I learned them well.

And even though most of those old people are gone now, and the communities we lost can never be found again, I know what I learned from all those stories: that no matter what happens, we can always make a new story. I look at all the women I see each day in Sandveld and I see that we have created new support systems, we have a kind of good neighbourliness which I haven't found anywhere else, and that is a story that I need to tell. I think of Annetjie and Irene and the way they have helped each other to learn, that's a story too. Charlene who was always ready to help out with a smile on her face, and Frances taking in lost children, and Rhoda looking after Isaac, and Sophie the Shebeen queen. So many stories.

CHAPTER TWENTY-SEVEN

I felt the drawing project was going well and the children were really starting to be much more observant in their drawing than they had been previously. Ironically, their drawings were also becoming much more creative than they had been, and I am sure you remember how cross I was when I was told by various people that the way I was teaching them was intervening too much and ruining their creativity. But now I could see that having learned to focus their vision carefully, and to really see the world around them, was allowing them to be more creative, not less.

Of course, Louise had something to say about all this. "There is a problem here," she said. "Your programme can't just be about looking, or just about art. The whole point of what I am trying to show you in this course is that if you teach kids some marvellous skills in one aspect of school learning, or even in a few school subjects, that is great, but it doesn't change their lives in any way. You have to take that skill, whatever it is you taught them, and make it real for them in their lives outside school.

"That is what really makes it meaningful: when you can go beyond that actual school lesson. You remember, we talked about what we call 'transcendence' in learning. It's not just about giving information or teaching a new skill, but about taking that information into another area, and making links with other aspects of their life. Any thinking skill a child learns must be something they can use all their lives, not just at school or at college."

She had talked about this before, in our lectures, but I think I hadn't grasped it properly.

I had spent weeks and weeks showing my class the cognitive skill of organisation. I was trying to help the kids apply this idea to a whole range of different areas, like organising things inside the class and outside, in the playground. Like helping Irene to organise her school bag and when to do her homework , and showing the kids how I organised our daily timetable, and how the daily register of who was at school and who was absent helped me organise the information I had to give to Frances. I had shown them how the builders of our new classrooms used organisation skills to plan the space for the classrooms, how big they should be and where to place them, and how they counted the bricks to make sure there were enough.

But that was all inside the school gates. I had not done enough to make the kids see that these ideas about organisation apply to their lives outside of school. I hadn't thought enough about how they apply to Patricia's work at the library and to the people planning our new school up the road.

But at least I now had support from someone who knew, from an expert in education, that I was on the right track. And now I was determined to show everyone what my kids could do, and I was going to make it public and invite everyone I knew, people from Sandveld but also all the teachers at Silverleaf and all those who had said I was somehow intervening too much with my kids through the way I was teaching them.

And I was going to do it outside the school gates.

* * *

There is a café, quite a high-society kind of place, in Kalk Bay right opposite the fishing harbour. People go there for coffee and home-baked bread but also to see and be seen. It is a place which I would never normally have gone to, it was just not my kind of place and not my kind of people, and anyway we didn't have that kind of money to pay for coffee and a piece of cake which we could get at a friend's house.

Peter, the artist who had helped us paint the wall, had once had an exhibition at that café. I remembered having gone to see his exhibition, with Frances and Patricia, and how, when we got there, we just couldn't make ourselves walk in, and we walked right past the door.

We turned round and walked past the door a second time, Frances and Patricia and I, before Patricia said, "Come on, this is ridiculous! It's a free country now!" and she marched into the café, followed hesitantly by Frances and even more so by me.

I remember how once, long ago, when I was about nine, I had a huge argument with Grandma Rachael, because I said why shouldn't I go into any shop, even if there is a sign saying 'Whites Only' on the door, and Grandma Rachael told me how childish I was to think that I, Dolores, a silly dreaming Coloured girl, could make up her own rules about how things worked in life.

Well, that was then, in the days of apartheid, and this was now, so really it was silly of us to even think we shouldn't go into the café, but my heart was beating thump thump thump in my chest anyway. Patricia sat down at a table near the exhibition wall and we looked at Peter's paintings of the sea and the *trek* fishermen, pulling their nets in. He had managed to show how the wind blows the sea spray and how the fishermen have a permanent squint because of trying to keep the sun and sand out of their eyes, and how they have to lean over with the weight of the net they are pulling in, and the excitement of the locals who have come to watch, to see what the nets bring in, and the cool, calculating expression on the face of the man who owns the boat and the nets when he checks how many edible fish he has caught and how much he can sell them for.

So that was the place I wanted to have our exhibition, to show our kids' pictures just like Peter had shown his, and to have everyone see our pictures while they were having their coffee and cake.

***

What I needed to plan carefully was how to persuade the café owner to show our pictures. He probably had hundreds of people wanting to use his walls for exhibitions, so why should he choose us? I know that a picture in a gallery has to be liked because it is art, and not because someone has worked hard to improve his drawing. And no matter how proud I was of my kids' work, I was not such a dreamer as to think that they were on the same level as those of a grown-up professional artist.

I thought that perhaps I would have to shock the café owner into looking at our work, so I started to put together a collection of pictures in pairs: before and after. That way he would see that even though those early drawings were very poor, the later ones, by the same child, were wonderful. So even though I know it was a bit sneaky of me, I chose the drawings of the five children who had made the most progress since the beginning of the drawing project.

I have to be honest and admit I did not choose Devlyn's drawings, because they were almost painful to look at: a few very faint scribbles, almost invisible, in a corner of the page, in one colour only. You could see he hadn't held the pencil firmly enough to even make a really visible mark; it was more like a chance result of a branch scratching on a windowpane in the wind.

Some of the other kids' drawings had more to look at: Mandisa's early drawings did have some clear marks, lines and scribbles, but they were all the same colour and didn't seem to represent anything. Of course, in her mind they may have had a lot of meaning; there was no way to know because in those days, at the beginning of the school year, I hadn't thought to ask the kids what they were drawing, or imagining. But when I placed it in my folder facing Mandisa's latest drawing, you would not have believed they were by the same child, with a time gap of only three months.

Mandisa had told me that her latest drawing was a picture of the wind. There were wavy shapes in the sky, and something like sand dunes coming up to meet them, and all sorts of objects which had been blown into the sky by the wind, whirling around and appearing suddenly: an upside-down bird, a hat, a newspaper. It was the very essence of movement and wind and I have never seen our own Cape wind, so familiar to all of us, represented so well.

As a final touch, Mandisa had spread glue over the page and sprinkled real sand over it, so that the texture was rough and sandy and scratchy, just like you feel if you have stood outside in the wind for too long.

Bongani's early drawings were a lot like what I had often seen in children age three who were just starting to draw: sun-like things, made up of circles with spikes radiating outwards. That was good, it said to me that he had been looking at the page while he was drawing, because you can't get the spikes in the right place, around the circle, if you don't look at them, but he had been four and a half when he drew them. Now, at four and three-quarters, his drawings were of people. There was a drawing of his family, with a very big dad, and a delicate, smaller mum, and he and his smaller brother, all in different sizes, and actually showing the different facial expressions of each person: Bongani himself smiling, the baby brother crying, mum worrying, and dad sleeping! The drawing was clearly telling a story, about how this family lived and how they related to each other. In the top right corner was a little figure, quite faintly drawn, and he told me that was granny who died long ago. So immediately I could see how important the memory of that granny was to the family, even now.

Before we started the drawing project, Mandisa and Bongani would have been considered, based on their early drawings, as children of rather low ability. Now their drawings took my breath away.

I collected pairs of drawings by a few more children, before and after, and placed them opposite each other in a big folder, so that the difference was clear to see. I then had ten pictures. Okay, Grandma Rachael, just watch me now. You will see what a dreamer can do when she starts to nag.

* * *

Patricia asked one of her many contacts to come and take a professional photo of each of the five 'artists'. I stuck the portraits of the children on the first page of the folder, with their first names and their ages, and made a title page which read 'SUNBEAMS PRESCHOOL' (written by Irene, of course, with each letter in a different colour) and then I was ready to go and persuade the café owner to let us use his exhibition wall.

I only allowed myself one heartbeat's hesitation before opening the door and marching in and asking to see the owner. I introduced myself as a local teacher, and said I had seen and enjoyed Peter's recent exhibition on the wall, and I had an idea for another exhibition. And I opened my display file to the page with Mandisa's wind drawing, knowing that it would be the most impressive.

The owner looked at it for a long time. He didn't say anything and didn't have any expression on his face and I began to get worried. Maybe he didn't want children's drawings, maybe I was mad to think this kind of thing could be compared to the art that Peter produced.

But slowly, he began to page through my album, and to look back at some of the drawings for a second time, and then he spent quite a while looking at the photos of the kids themselves.

And then he asked me if it would suit us (if it would *suit* us?) to have the exhibition in three weeks' time, because his wall was booked up for the next few weeks but by the middle of June it would be free. He offered us the use of his wall for a full week, seven whole days.

There were a few things to decide, like how to hang the pictures on the wall. Framing was out of the question, we didn't have any money to spend. Once again, Helen, the lady with the stationery business, came to the rescue and had frames cut out of thick cardboard, and as all our drawings were done on the back of used computer printouts, they were all the same size, so it was easy to just glue the cardboard frames on the pictures. We decided to use double-sided tape to stick the pictures on the wall. The simplest way was the best, we didn't want to pretend to be anything other than what we were: a group of kids from the poorest community in the area, who had spent time and effort really looking at the world around them, and had taken the trouble to show us in their drawings not only what they saw but also what they felt.

***

I started a campaign to tell as many people as possible about the exhibition. I asked Frances and Lorraine to send out emails to all the people they knew, and Patricia to call in all her many volunteers to tell them they should do themselves a favour and go and have a cup of coffee in Kalk Bay and look at our art. I asked the Trust to contact all their donors, even those in the UK, to tell them that it was a good time to come to Cape Town, winter is sometimes not so bad in Cape Town, and they would enjoy having coffee opposite the harbour and seeing some art.

And, of course, I also invited the teachers from Silverleaf, as well as some of the parents I had met on my days there.

I invited all my classmates at university, and Louise promised to tell all the lecturers in the Teacher Training department, and even to arrange to bring some of them in her car on the day she was coming to visit our exhibition. She was also keen to visit me at Sunbeams, to see what I was doing there. Well, I tell you, I was a bit less keen on that, it felt like an exam and I wasn't ready for it, but it was too late to take back my invitation and anyway I had obviously been so excited when I told her about it that I had managed to enthuse her too and she was going to come, whether I wanted it or not.

CHAPTER TWENTY-EIGHT

Two weeks before the exhibition at the café a new crisis hit us, just out of the blue.

I am sure you read about it, the xenophobia attacks on foreigners, on people from Zimbabwe and the Congo and Somalia who had come to live here in South Africa. Maybe you didn't hear about it if you were still in London at the time.

It seems that some people here were angry with these foreigners, and thought they were taking away jobs from local people. Personally I think the whole thing was to do with some criminals who felt their territory was being trespassed on. But somehow it caught on and foreign Black people were being attacked all around the country. Some were murdered. One was set alight in the street and people laughed as he died.

Charlene was from Zimbabwe, and when Martinus showed her the newspaper she panicked. Luckily it was after school and Irene was already sitting in Frances' office. Charlene grabbed her, ran to her house to pick up some warm clothes and a blanket and was gone. We didn't even have time to ask her where she was going, and all the kids in my class were obviously aware something bad was happening and I had to try to calm them down, so I couldn't go and ask anyone or check up on Charlene and Irene.

Later, after school, I went to Charlene's house to ask about them, but none of the neighbours knew where they had gone.

When the South-Easter wind blows, bringing us all that sand from the beach, it knows exactly in which direction it is going, but it seems that with people things are not so easy, and everyone just scattered in different directions.

Frances tried to phone Charlene but her phone just rang and rang. Charlene did not come to school the next day. I was beside myself with worry and I still had to teach, and try not to alarm my kids, who by then had heard enough to know something bad was happening.

I was consumed with fear – not only for Irene and the foreign and refugee kids in South Africa, but all of them, Isaac and Devlyn and the whole class. How would they survive all this violence? It is not something occasional, it is part of their daily lives. Sometimes, on a Monday, you can see that the kids have had a hard weekend, they have seen things they shouldn't have seen, when their parents or neighbours have been drunk and violent. Sometimes it takes a whole day to calm a child down so that he can learn. How could our Sandveld parents still be warm, loving, protective, when they themselves were not protected from this? And where would Devlyn be in ten years' time, at age fourteen, when other kids of that age are already experimenting with drugs and trying to resist the attractions of joining a gang?

* * *

It wasn't only Charlene and Irene who were missing. By the next day about a third of the kids at Sunbeams were not at school. Ironically we had a few very easy teaching days, because the children were so unusually quiet, and unlike our usually crowded conditions there was suddenly a lot of space. We regretted every single time we had complained about the lack of space, or with we could have either bigger classrooms or fewer kids.

Frances spent hours on the phone, trying to find the families, to ask if they were alright and to ask the parents if they needed food or blankets. She finally got an answer on Charlene's phone and Charlene told us she and Irene had gone to the house of her husband's former employer, who had always been kind to them even though her husband had gone missing that time when he was on the run from the police. They were hiding in the employer's garage – he had a big garage and only one car, so there was a little space for Charlene and Irene to put out some blankets and cushions. They thought they would stay there a few days until things got better, but to tell the truth nobody knew if things would get better and we were pleased that at least they were safe. But I hated the thought of them spending their day in a tiny dark space and sleeping on a cold hard concrete floor.

Later that day Martinus took Bertha and me to the house where they were hiding and we brought them food, some more blankets, and some books and toys for Irene, as well as her school bag, which she had left in my classroom in the rush to get away.

I hoped they would be safe there, and would stay a day or two, but the next day, who should turn up at Sunbeams but Charlene, with Irene walking close beside her, both of them carrying the piles of blankets and books and all the stuff they had taken to their place of safety.

"That man, he says we can't stay there any more, he doesn't want to take the risk, we had nowhere to go, so we came back. What will happen will happen," said Charlene. "We got nowhere else to hide now."

So in the morning, once all the children had arrived, we locked the front gate of the school and Martinus parked his car right in front of our front door so that nobody could get in without carefully squeezing through, and we locked the classroom doors and got on with our day. The police were patrolling in the streets and we just hoped for the best.

Slowly, in the next few days, the foreign children started trickling back to school and a few days later they were all back. And although we read in the papers about the awful attacks that had happened in other places in the country, the fact is that in Sandveld not a single person was attacked. It is true that the police were driving up and down the streets all day and all night just in case, but actually they didn't have anything to do. Somehow, in spite of everything that goes wrong in Sandveld, there is something special here: something protected us in those bad days.

* * *

By the time the day of the exhibition dawned, the attacks had stopped and the country had mostly calmed down a bit, although in some areas, like in Masi township on the other side of the Peninsula and in the northern areas of the country, hundreds of people of all ages, even small children, who had come to South Africa from other countries in Africa were still staying in temporary camps, protected by the police. Sleeping all together in huge tents, without sufficient toilets, and in some cases running short of drinking water. And everyone was talking about the risks of cholera and TB in those crowded conditions, and then there were a few days of cold and the rain, and how would these people survive?

But in Sandveld all was calm. The kids came to school on the day of the exhibition really excited. We had asked the school in Kalk Bay, the one which lent us their bus for the botanical gardens visit, to lend us their bus again to take the kids to see their exhibition; we were determined that the exhibition would not be just for visitors, but for the kids themselves to see what they had achieved.

The wall at the café in Kalk Bay was quite small, certainly not big enough to put up a picture by each of my thirty-six children, let alone a 'before' and an 'after' picture, so I had set up an additional exhibition, where I could hang a picture by every single child. I got permission from the local supermarket just next to Sandveld, where we bought stuff daily and whose staff knew us, to let us use one of their huge walls, and I asked each child to choose from his folder of pictures that he had produced over the months the one he liked best, and their personal favourites were the ones we showed at that supermarket exhibition.

The bus took us to the supermarket, where the kids behaved beautifully after I had given them a little talk about the rules of going to exhibitions: you have to be very quiet, because people want to look at the pictures in silence so that they can think about how lovely your pictures are. And you have to wait your turn, because we can't have thirty-six children running into a shop at the same time. And because the kids were now used to following rules after all the hopscotch we had been playing, they knew exactly what I meant and they behaved perfectly. Many of the parents were waiting at the supermarket when we arrived in our bus (a trip which took no more than five minutes from our school) and the pride on their faces was something to see.

After about half an hour, the supermarket staff brought drinking yoghurt and a banana for each child, which was a wonderful and unexpected surprise. Then it was back on the bus for the slightly longer trip to Kalk Bay and the café.

All of our kids had been to our local beach, the one near Sandveld, because it was not a very long walk from the school across Sandveld's sand dunes to the sea, but very few had ever been to Kalk Bay, and the boats and the shops were something quite new for them. Their eyes got bigger and bigger; they didn't know where to look first. Frances and I got them out of the bus and onto the harbour wall so they could watch people fishing, and I took six at a time across the road to the café to look at the exhibition.

There were lots of people in the café, some of whom I recognised from Silverleaf, and my lecturer Louise with a few of her colleagues, and also some customers of the cafe who hadn't known about the exhibition but were having coffee and pastries there anyway and who were curious to know who were the kids in these lovely photos, and how their drawings came to be exhibited on the wall. Luckily, Helen had told me I should write the story of the exhibition and describe our 'Learning to Look and Looking to Learn' project on a piece of card to put up next to the exhibition, so I didn't have to explain to anyone and I could be virtually anonymous, shepherding my groups of wonderful children, six at a time, in and out.

Even though it was already winter, it was one of those perfect Cape Town days when the clouds roll away and the wind disappears and the sun is warm but not hot, and I looked at the beautiful scenes of my kids' art on the wall, as well as across the road where the fishing boats were coming in and people were starting to gather to buy fresh fish, or walking along the jetty with their little buckets and their home-made fishing rods, hoping to catch something in the deep seas just on the other side of the harbour wall.

***

It should have been wonderful. But it's a strange thing, because for some reason, I can't explain it, that night I suddenly felt a huge exhaustion and emptiness.

This was in spite of the fact that the exhibition was, for my kids and for our school, a real triumph, where we proved to everyone that our kids can do things as well as or better than anyone else, no matter what school they go to and no matter how deprived our township. We got a special letter of thanks and congratulations from the Sandveld Development Trust and another letter from the funders overseas in London, and Frances and Patricia and Annetjie were just glowing with pride and happiness. And the kids were so proud of themselves, they couldn't stop talking about how their pictures were "on the wall of that supermarket, and that place there in Kalk Bay, you know, where you can go fishing".

But I couldn't get it out of my mind: but for pure luck, or fate or whatever, Charlene and Irene and plenty of others could have been killed in those xenophobia attacks. And even though nothing had happened in Sandveld, there was a mood going around the country and who knew, it could start up again at any time.

And even though Charlene and Irene were alright now, who knew how long Charlene could go on, with her illness. And what would happen to Irene then?

Somehow my mood attached itself, like the sand blown in a gale, to everything around me. Even thinking about Devlyn and his progress, and how Annetjie's life had changed, didn't help me to stop thinking about all those thousands who were not at Sunbeams, who didn't have a Frances or a Sandveld Trust to take care of their housing and food and clothes.

The enormity of the problem got to me and I suddenly felt, I can't do this anymore, it is just too hard. The problems are too enormous, this thing has been going on for nearly four hundred years, who am I to think that I, or any teacher, or even lots of teachers, can make any difference? I felt a big despair setting in, like the clouds from the North-Wester wind, and I lost my optimism and my ability to think never mind how hard it is today, Dolores, tomorrow will be better. I just lost that.

And that's when I started thinking about finding a different job, somewhere that I could earn a bit more money and not take everyone's sad story home with me each night, somewhere that I could feel, at the end of a week, that I have done a good job and now I can have a good rest and not worry about anything at all, all weekend. And think about my own child first, without having to think of everyone else's child.

***

Don't think I just gave up, just like that. I stuck to my plans in the classroom. There were days when it was hard to get out of bed, when I just wanted to hide away and think about nothing, but I got up every day and went to work because I had no choice.

I kept on working with my kids, trying to follow the Cognitive Education ideas but also trying something a bit different: I was determined not to just ignore those terrifying few days of the xenophobia but to try to make sense of it for my kids. So we sat in a circle and each child had to say something kind, something nice, to the child on his right, and we went round the circle saying kind things. Some kids said things like "I like your T-shirt" and the next few copied that because they couldn't think of anything else to say, but gradually, as we went round and round and I asked them to think what they would like a child to say to them, what would make them feel happy, they started coming up with things like "You have got nice eyes" or "I like to play with you" or "You are my friend".

I also got them comparing themselves to each other. I put two children side by side and the others had to compare then. We talked openly about differences, like height, hair length and skin colour, and talking different languages at home, and having lived in different countries before they came to Sandveld, but we also talked about similarities, like both having a nice smile, and both liking to play hopscotch, and both wearing warm clothes because it is cold outside.

When you practise that cognitive skill of comparing, you have to make sure to compare what is the same, as well as what is different. That's a rule in Cognitive Education.

CHAPTER TWENTY-NINE

Charlene was getting more and more tired. Frances and the Trust insisted that she stop working, and she still got her salary, and she got all the medication she needed, but somehow she was not doing well, she was getting thinner and thinner.

So it was not a huge surprise, although it was with huge sadness, when one day she called all of us together and told us she had made a decision. She was going to go and live with her mother, in Delft, which is a huge sprawling township about an hour from Sandveld, and her mother, Irene's Granny Sylvia, was going to help Charlene take care of Irene. "Just in case", she said, "you don't know how this thing will get me."

We had met Granny Sylvia on a few occasions when she had come to visit Charlene and Irene, and we knew her to be a strong, capable woman, who worked hard cleaning people's houses and who would be a wonderful carer for her daughter and granddaughter. She was one of those women of Africa who just take things on, who seem to have a limitless capacity to care for others and to still stand strong and sing out loud in church every Sunday.

But we felt devastated at losing Charlene and Irene, who had both become part of our Sunbeams family. I had spent so many hours with Irene, sometimes just chatting to her, helping her to read, planning the shoe charity and watching her help Annetjie in turn, I felt as if I was losing my own daughter. But it was the right decision for them and at the end of the week we had a big party, with lots of laughter and lots of tears, and we said goodbye, *totsiens*, see you soon, don't be a stranger, come and visit *hey*! And Irene promised to write letters, to me and to Annetjie, because (she told me privately) she wanted to make sure Annetjie was still reading even if Irene, her teacher, was not around to encourage her.

And Isaac also moved on: we decided that he really did need to be with kids his own age, and that he would soon catch up on the work they had been doing, and if necessary we could arrange for him to get some extra tutoring with one of the reading scheme volunteers, so that when he started First Grade he would be up to their level.

There was a big gap in my day without Irene and Isaac. But I had Annetjie and Devlyn and the whole class, and every evening and weekend I had to spend hours writing up my university assignments for Louise: a long paper on my 'Learning to Look' programme and another one tracking Devlyn's progress. She asked my permission to print my 'Learning to Look' report in the teaching department newsletter, which she circulated to a group of teachers and lecturers who were promoting Cognitive Education all over South Africa.

* * *

I can look at the work we did over the last year and feel proud. I am proud of Annetjie and Charlene, who by joining our teaching staff not only changed the quality of our teaching completely and helped our children to grow and to learn, but also changed their own lives for the better.

I am proud of Isaac, who went through three operations and months of pain and was still standing, still learning, still explaining to me how to do things.

I am proud of Devlyn, who started to sit still, to concentrate, to focus on some activities like Lego and puzzles, is talking more in class and can now count to ten.

I am proud of our art exhibition and of the wall outside the school which our children decorated so beautifully, and they are proud of how our school looks with its new classrooms and its tidied-up playground equipment and the hopscotch games painted on the paving.

I know there are still problems and our town has got its fair share of crime and violence and drugs and sadness. But we have also got something to be proud of, we have not sat still and just done nothing, we have been busy and we have made something happen here.

We provide a safe place for kids to spend their day, and get good food, and learn; the library has its doors open to all kids every afternoon, just to come and sit with Patricia and feel her warmth and maybe practise their reading. Lots of kids have now got shoes that fit properly. There are the 1600 houses, and the new school. It's our own little world, and here we do our work.

***

I still had one more assignment to hand in before I could get my diploma, the one about my personal and family history. But I just could not do it. I hadn't found the other assignments too difficult to write, even though they took hours and hours, but this one was beyond me.

I spent weeks thinking about it, but the thing was, as I told you, I couldn't find anything about my family other than what I already knew: the names of Grandma Rachael and a few of my uncles and aunts. There were no records, and everyone who might have known something had died.

And to talk about the history of the Coloured people, well it has all been said already, there are some wonderful books about us, some by sociologists and some by politicians and educators, and even some wonderful fiction which tells stories about District Six and about people who were involved in the Struggle during apartheid times. So what could I possibly add to that?

Louise was worried, because she was determined that I should get my diploma, and we met a few times and she tried to help me to come to some personal conclusions about my own identity, knowing what I now knew about the history. We talked about how I felt about the Prestwich Street events and its memorial, and the hours I had spent visiting the District Six Museum and learning about what life had been like there, and how people felt when they were evicted, and all the research I had read about slavery.

But I couldn't come up with anything. Each time I read an article or a book on the subject of Coloured identity, I found myself agreeing with that writer, even though many of them had ideas which were totally opposed to each other.

Well, maybe that's a conclusion too.

Everyone has a different point of view about this, and they are all important ideas. So many ideas, so many opinions. It's a bit like beach sand. Sand can be something you see all around you, every day, and try to ignore, and it can be irritating grains blown in your face by the South-Easter gales. Or it can be a beach, or a school playground.

Our Cape beaches are famous for their velvety soft sand. But if you pick up a handful of sand on the beach and look carefully, using your eyes or even better a magnifying glass, you will see your hand is holding differently shaped grains in different colours.

I looked it up in one of the encyclopaedias in Patricia's library. Our beach sand is made up of grains of whitish limestone, bits of seashell in tan and brown and blue from the mussels which live on our coast, some pink grains of coral, and some tiny pieces of black and grey granite. Each grain is a different size and a different shape. When you see the grains all lumped together, they all look about the same. But on their own, each one is unique.

***

Still, you can't write a research paper for university by talking about sand, so I didn't do it, and I didn't complete the course and I didn't get my diploma.

So now I have told you all about myself and about Sunbeams, and lots of stories about Sandveld. I don't know if you think it is a good place, or a hard place, or just a place like any other. We have our bad people, we have our troubles, and we have our good people and our good times. We have lots of fun at Sunbeams, and even though it is hard work, we feel good about it.

Our new classrooms are ready, the new primary school building will be completed soon, and Isaac will be one of the first children to go to that school and we are all very excited about it.

But now, to get back to the present, you have been interviewing me for this job, and it is a good job, and it is a good salary, don't get me wrong, and I am sorry I took up so much of your time. Grandma Rachael always told me, "My girl, *meisie*, you speak too much! Always talking, talking, talking."

But I have decided, thank you very much, I actually don't want to change jobs, I want to be a teacher in Sandveld.

So I am staying. I think what I want is to be the person in my family who makes things continue, who has an idea and can keep it going and pass it on.

I'm not saying that the past, and history, are not important, I'm just saying that if you can't find out your history, then you have to make your identity from something else. For me, the past isn't available to examine or to know. I can't lean on the past, or even see the past. All I have is now. What I do, who I live with, who I teach. The people I see in Sandveld every day, and our strong bonds with each other.

So what I have now will just have to do. Maybe one day, maybe in twenty or even forty years' time, this now, this present time, will be a past for Devlyn and Irene and Isaac, and they will remember how we painted the wall, and cleaned the street, and played hopscotch, and learned how to learn.

THE END

USEFUL REFERENCES

Adhikari, M. (2005) *Not White Enough, Not Black Enough: Racial Identity in the South African Coloured Community.* Double Story Books, Cape Town.

Adikhari, M. (2009) (Ed.) *Burdened by Race: Coloured Identities in Southern Africa.* [Especially Chapter 3, Trauma and Memory, by Henry Trotter] UCT Press, Cape Town.

Bruner, J. (1974) *Toward a Theory of Instruction.* Belknap Press.

Bradley, R., Caldwell, B., Rock, S., Casey, P. and Nelson, J. (1987) *The early development of low birth weight infants: relationship to health, family status, family context, family processes and parenting.* International Journal of Behavioral Development, 10, pp 301-318.

Dawes, A. and Donald, D. (Eds) (1994) *Childhood and Adversity: Psychological Perspectives from South African Research.* [Especially relevant in writing this book were Chapter 1, *Understanding the Psychological Consequences of Adversity*, by Dawes and Donald; and Chapter 4, *Malnutrition and Psychological Development*, by Linda Richter and Raoul Griesel] David Philip, Cape Town.

Erasmus, Zimitri. (2001) *Coloured by History, Shaped by Place.* (Accessed online 24.04.2014) http://www2. warwick.ac.uk/fac/soc/sociology/rsw/current/cscs/creole_bibliography/intro_z._erasmus.pdf

Feuerstein, Reuven, Rand, Y., Hoffman, M.B., and Miller, R. (1980/2004) *Instrumental Enrichment. An Intervention Programme for Cognitive Modifiability.* University Park Press, Baltimore, MD.

Haywood, H. C., Brooks, P. H. and Burns, S. (1992) *Bright Start: Cognitive Curriculum for Young Children.* Charlesbridge Publishers, Watertown, MA.

Hepner, R. and Maiden, N. (1977) *Growth rate, nutrient intake and 'mothering' as determinants of malnutrition in disadvantaged children.* Nutrition Reviews, 29, pp 219-223.

Mentis, M., Dunn-Bernstein, M., Mentis, M. and Skuy, M. (2009) *Bridging Learning: Unlocking Cognitive Potential In and Out of the Classroom.* Corwin Publishers.

Sharron, H. and Coulter, M. (2006) *Changing Children's Minds.* Imaginative Minds, Birmingham.

Tzuriel, D. (2013) *Mediated learning experience strategies and cognitive modifiability.* Journal of Cognitive Education and Psychology, 13, pp 59-80.

Wilson, F. and Ramphele, M. (1989) *Uprooting Poverty: The South African Challenge.* Creda Press, South Africa.

* * *

The District Six Museum (25 Buitenkant Street, Cape Town, South Africa) provides extensive information on some of the topics covered here, including oral histories of the Coloured community and the consequences of the Group Areas Act referred to in this book.

Printed in August 2021
by Rotomail Italia S.p.A., Vignate (MI) - Italy